"Do you think you'll be leaving when your year is up?"

"I may stay here until I have a long, gray beard."

"You looked good with a beard. I was sorry to see you'd shaved it," Jenny said with a half smile.

It was the first really personal thing she'd said to him. He felt gratified that she might see him as a man, not just as a minister.

"Maybe sometime we can get together just to talk—you know, without food," Mac said.

To his immense relief, Jenny smiled.

"I'm afraid you'd find my conversation pretty dull. I've never done anything the least bit adventurous compared to you."

Did his job as minister intimidate her? Mac wished he knew more about her. He had a feeling she'd make a very good friend to anyone she liked and trusted. Every instinct he had told him that she was as beautiful inside as she was to his eyes.

"You didn't say no?" he asked hopefully.

"No, I didn't say no." She gathered up their plates and started walking toward the kitchen.

She hadn't said yes, ei

Books by Pam Andrews

Love Inspired

Hometown Reunion
The Marriage Mission

PAM ANDREWS

is the mother-daughter writing team of Pam Hanson and Barbara Andrews. Barbara makes her home with Pam and her family in Nebraska. They have written numerous books for such publishers as Steeple Hill Books and Guideposts. Pam's background is in journalism, and she and her college professor husband have two sons. Barbara, the mother of four and grandmother of seven, also writes articles and a column about collectible postcards. Pam writes about faith and family at www.pamshanson.blogspot.com.

The Marriage Mission
Pam Andrews

Steeple
Hill®

Published by Steeple Hill Books™

STEEPLE HILL BOOKS

Steeple
Hill®

Recycling programs
for this product may
not exist in your area.

ISBN-13: 978-0-373-87599-3

THE MARRIAGE MISSION

Copyright © 2010 by Pamela Hanson and Barbara Andrews

Printed in U.S.A.

A generous man will prosper; he who refreshes others will himself be refreshed.
—*Proverbs* 11:25

This book is lovingly dedicated in memory of Patricia (Tricia) Larsen whose work for the poor and hungry of the world inspired us to create our hero.

Chapter One

Mac Arnett parked his vintage VW in front of Pleasantville, West Virginia's only barbershop, but the sign on the door didn't bode well. He got out of the car to read it, hoping it only meant that the barber had taken a short break.

"It's a boy! Grandpa Charley will be back Monday."

Good news for the new grandfather was bad news for Mac. He needed a haircut now, not five days from now, and he'd already checked the phone book. Charley's was the only barbershop in town.

He couldn't go to a job interview looking like a wild man, although that's pretty much what he'd become in his years of overseas missions. He could scrape off his scruffy beard himself, but experience told him that cutting his own shoulder-length hair would be a comic disaster.

The main business district extended for several blocks with bright, striped awnings in front of many of the shops. Big vase-shaped cement planters were empty now, but it was early April, too soon for flowers. He looked in both directions, at a loss what to do next.

Pleasantville was nestled in a valley, the wooded hillsides just beginning to show the green tinge of budding trees. Mac shivered a little, realizing that he needed more than a T-shirt in spite of the bright sunshine. After his time in East Africa, Haiti and Guatemala, he would have to get used to a cooler clime.

He thought of his last mission assignment, rebuilding a church destroyed by a Guatemalan mudslide. He worried about the good people he'd left there, but the church board had recalled him to the States with good reason. After three surgeries in Cleveland on a broken ankle that hadn't been set properly, he was more than eager to answer a new call.

On the surface, Pleasantville seemed to live up to its name, but Mac had grown up not far from here, the son of a dedicated minister. Underneath the cheerful facade, life could be hard for many in the West Virginia hills. The men did grueling, dangerous work in the coal mines with the specter of poverty always present if a mine closed.

At first Mac resisted the idea of continuing his ministry in his own country, but long hours of prayer and contemplation had eased most of his doubts. His faith had been honed by his years of missionary work since graduating from the seminary, and he was ready to serve wherever he could.

First he had to convince a church committee that he was at least partially civilized. It would take more than a new suit and a shave. He had to get rid of the Tarzan look by getting his long mane of dark brown hair cut off.

He started walking down the sidewalk, gratified that the twinge of pain in his ankle wasn't severe anymore. Across the street he saw a particularly colorful awning with pink and yellow stripes. He squinted into the sun and read the sign painted in gold on the large front window: Charlene's Beauty Salon.

He grinned and decided it was worth a shot.

More people were inside the shop than outside on the sidewalks, and ladies in bright pink capes occupied three of the four chairs. Mac went up to a reception desk and waited until one of the beauticians left her client and came up to him.

"What can I do for you today?" she asked with a broad grin that could be interpreted as friendly—or slightly amused, considering that he was the only male in the place.

"Is there any chance of getting a haircut? I tried the barbershop, but it's closed."

"Oh, yeah, Charley finally got a grandson. Bet he's excited. His first four grandkids were girls. Funny isn't it, how boys run in some families and girls in others."

"About a haircut…"

"Sure, we can take you if you don't mind waiting a little while. Jenny, when will you be done?" she called over to a tall willowy young woman wearing the shop's uniform of dark slacks and a pink tunic.

"Ten minutes or so, Charlene," she said with the slight drawl that only a native West Virginian would be likely to detect.

"Have a seat, and Jenny will be with you as soon as she can."

Mac perched on a low chair upholstered in a silvery fabric and took stock of his surroundings. Charlene, probably the owner and boss, was a heavyset woman with yellow hair piled on her head in layers like a wedding cake. The third beautician, combing out tight curls on a blue-haired elderly woman at the rear of the shop, looked as if she'd colored her hair with a crayon, an especially vivid purple one.

Mac had felt more comfortable in a Mayan hut with a

dirt floor. The sinks, chairs and work surfaces in the shop were all a glossy black. Everything else seemed to be pink, even the tiles on the floor. He let his eyes wander to the young woman who was going to cut his hair, Jenny. He was good at remembering names, a skill that would serve him well if he was chosen to lead the Pleasantville congregation.

He had a feeling he was in good hands with Jenny. Unlike the other two, she'd left her hair a natural-looking dark honey blond, swept away from her face to fall in waves in back.

With nothing else to do, he found himself studying her face whenever it was turned toward him. Her brow was high and smooth with straight, even eyebrows not plucked too thin. Her face was oval with even features, although her nose was more classical than cute, reminding him of the profile on the ancient Roman coin his father had given to him when he started at the seminary. He used it when he preached about the widow's mite.

"It won't be long now," a melodious voice said, interrupting his musings.

He smiled at Jenny and assured her that he wasn't in a hurry, although in truth, he was eager to get back to his motel room. He needed to shower and shave before his interview, and he hoped for some time to pray and consider his vocation.

He shifted uncomfortably on the chair, wondering whether he'd gotten so used to sitting cross-legged on the ground that it would be hard to get used to furniture again.

Jenny worked quietly, unlike her two coworkers who carried on nonstop conversations while they did their jobs. He was grateful that he'd drawn the least talkative.

He didn't want to say anything about why he was here in Pleasantville, not until he received and accepted a call from the First Bible Church. It would be unprofessional and, worse, he knew how rumors raced through a small town.

Ten minutes passed like an hour, and he tried not to look at his watch too often. At last Jenny escorted her beaming client to the reception desk and checked her out.

"I can take you now, sir," she said.

"Mac, my name is Mac."

He was going to have to get used to being called Reverend Arnett, but he wasn't going to start today.

"I'm Jenny," she said and smiled.

He remembered her name but didn't say so.

"If you'll just take a chair," she said, indicating the one just vacated.

She swept up the hair around her chair with an economy of movement that was both graceful and thorough, then went to a sink at the back to wash her hands.

"Now, what would you like?" she asked, wrapping a strip of paper around his neck, then enveloping him in one of the pink nylon capes and fastening it at the back.

"Short and neat," he said catching a glimpse of his scruffy face in the big mirror in front of him.

What did she see when she looked at him? His blue eyes had dark shadows, souvenirs of several sleepless nights trying to decide whether Pleasantville was the place for him. When had he last shaved? He couldn't remember, but it was going to be a chore to get rid of the beard that always came in darker than his brown hair. Was this a face that a West Virginia congregation would trust to lead them? He thought of his father's silvery gray hair; warm, caring eyes and compassionate face and had his doubts.

"I have to warn you, I haven't cut many men's hair," she said earnestly. "Some of the high school girls were getting really short cuts a few years ago. I'll have to go by that."

"I'm sure you'll do fine."

He caught a glimpse of her eyes in the mirror but failed to decide what color they were. At first he thought they were green, but flecks of yellow and brown threw him off. Maybe they were hazel, he decided for lack of a word to adequately describe them.

"I'll cut for length first," she said, pushing down a plunger on a bottle that he assumed was water since it didn't add to the already pungent smells in the shop.

He watched her hands as she worked, fascinated by the sure snips of her scissors. His hair tumbled to the floor, leaving stray clumps clinging to the cape.

He felt awkward, sitting there swathed in pink in a ladies' beauty parlor, and wasn't sure where to focus his gaze. When he caught her eyes in the mirror, she looked away quickly, so he kept watching her hands. Her fingers were long and slender and unadorned by rings. Of course, she could have taken them off to work, but he didn't see a telltale indentation on her left-hand ring finger. Not that it was any of his concern. He might never see her again, especially if things didn't work out with the church committee.

Jenny hadn't been nervous about a haircut since her first few tries in beauty school, and that had been ages ago. Well, nearly eight years, but sometimes it seemed that she'd been doing hair forever, not that she didn't like her job. Charlene was a fair and considerate boss, and Nadine was fun with her fads and fancies, although she'd perhaps gone too far with purple hair. The older women who patronized the shop were having doubts about Nadine, but she managed to keep busy with younger clients.

Why did she feel odd cutting this man's hair? He was a stranger who'd only come into the shop because Charley's was closed. It was unlikely she'd ever see him again. And he certainly wasn't picky. He'd pretty much left the styling up to her, and she usually had confidence in what she was doing.

Maybe it was because he was watching every snip of her scissors in the mirror, though she couldn't fault him for that. There wasn't anything else to do during a haircut. She would much rather do someone else's hair than have to sit still to have hers done.

"Feels like spring today," he said.

"Warm weather is welcome. We had a hard winter."

She answered automatically, but she did prefer a neutral topic to the gossip that Charlene loved. Jenny sometimes suspected that the business would suffer if it weren't a conduit for all the news in town. With only a weekly newspaper, people relied on word of mouth to know what was going on.

"Do you like the part on the right or left?" she asked, still trying to decide the best way to style it.

He laughed softly. "I can't remember the last time I parted it on either side. You can decide."

What kind of man was indifferent to his looks? In her experience, even the scruffy ones thought they were making some kind of statement by the way they wore their hair. Her ex-brother-in-law once did thirty days in the county jail for DUI. He was furious when the sheriff forced him to get a haircut before he served his time and insulted because the lawman implied that it was to keep lice out of his prison.

The sure way to ruin her day was to start thinking

about Duane and the way he'd left her sister, Sandy. She smiled at her client's image in the mirror and concentrated on giving him the best possible cut.

"There, how's that?" she asked, handing him a round hand mirror to see the back.

"Fine, you did a good job."

She hoped he wasn't just being polite. Without knowing anything about him, she'd been hard-pressed to choose between a short, casual cut or something more sophisticated. He had hair a lot of her clients would envy: a warm sable brown with no thinning or split ends. She was satisfied with the style that took advantage of a tendency to curl and hoped he was.

She was good at reading hair and guessed he was in his early thirties. What she couldn't figure out was why he was in Pleasantville. If they were hiring at the mine, Charlene would've been the first to know. Her husband, Ed, was a foreman, and she monitored the employment picture with intensity, worrying about his livelihood and the prospects for her business if it closed.

Jenny removed the pink cape, wishing that her boss had some alternative colors. Of course, most of their male customers were under ten, but some of them were known to protest the "silly" cape.

At the counter, she rang up his payment on a cash register that was fifty years out of date and protested when he added an additional five dollars as a tip.

"Really, it's too much," she said.

"I can't tell you how much I appreciate the cut. I hardly recognize myself." He smiled broadly and left, leaving the five-dollar bill on the counter.

Charlene came up beside Jenny while she waited to do the next step in a perm.

"He sure was handsome," the older woman said in a soft voice. "Wonder what he's doing here?"

"No idea," she replied, shrugging.

Jenny knew her boss—and friend—was angling for some bit of gossip to pass on to other clients, but Charlene knew Jenny wasn't one to pry into other people's business.

"What am I going to do with you?" Charlene teased. "A genuine, living, breathing hunk sets himself down in your chair, and you don't even find out where he's from."

Jenny smiled but shook her head. Charlene meant well, but she was a born matchmaker. She wouldn't rest until she heard wedding bells, but it wasn't going to happen.

Jenny had no intention of ever again being abandoned by a man. She'd expected to marry her high school boyfriend, Jack Henderson, but he'd left town with a promise to keep in touch that he never fulfilled. She'd also suffered along with her mother and her sister when their husbands deserted them, and she could get along fine without a man in her life. As far as she knew, falling for a man only led to a world of hurt.

Charlene returned to her perm, and Nadine checked out her client, then followed Jenny to the small lounge at the rear where the owner kept a pot of coffee and a small fridge with soda.

"Girl, who was that handsome guy in your chair?" the younger woman asked, sinking down on the sofa with a can of cola.

"Just someone passing through, as far as I know." Jenny checked her watch to confirm that she had ten minutes before her next appointment.

"I wish he'd been in my chair," Nadine sighed. "I hated to see those long locks go, though. I love a man who isn't afraid to let his hair grow. Maybe he was a rock star traveling incognito. Or a surfer dude chasing down big waves."

"In West Virginia?" Jenny asked, unable to hold back a smile.

"Did you see his car?" Nadine kicked off her high wooden-soled wedgies and wiggled her toes. "You can tell a lot about a man from what he drives."

"I didn't see it."

"I would've snuck a look out the window when he left."

"Never crossed my mind," Jenny said, helping herself to a diet soda. "But if he comes again, you can take care of him."

"I should be so lucky!" Nadine said dramatically.

Jenny shook her head at her coworker's enthusiasm. She didn't expect to see the new customer again, but she was curious about his reason for being in Pleasantville. They didn't see very many strangers, especially not men who hadn't had a haircut in ages. She wondered what he looked like without the heavy beard, but probably she'd never find out.

Chapter Two

$\sim$

Mac sipped the weak coffee that the church committee had served, missing the rich, full flavor of Guatemalan beans. He'd brought home a good supply, not only to help the impoverished farmers but also because it was delicious.

"I noted that you're single, Reverend Arnett," the spokesperson said. "Tell me, do you have any matrimonial plans in the future?"

Mrs. Hodges was a large, square-faced woman with iron-gray hair and friendly blue eyes that reflected a caring personality. His guess was that she was also one of the wealthiest members of the congregation, judging by her well-tailored navy suit and the multitude of rings on her fingers.

"I'd like nothing better than to marry and start a family of my own, but at the moment I don't have any plans."

"We've never had a minister who wasn't married," she said, frowning slightly. "Of course, it's not exactly a requirement. Now, does anyone else have any questions? Miss Dunning?"

Mac remembered that she was the Sunday school director. Rail thin with fluffy blond hair, she looked timid but her question was pointed.

"How long do you think you would stay as our minister?" she asked.

"I try to serve the Lord wherever He calls me. I'm afraid that's the best answer I can give you."

He'd expected that question but realized his answer might not satisfy a congregation eager to hire a permanent replacement for their retired minister.

"That sounds reasonable to me." Mr. Johnson was a roly-poly car salesman with unfortunate taste in sports jackets, but he radiated goodwill.

"Mr. Hadley?" Mrs. Hodges said, calling on an especially quiet member of the committee, a silver-haired, no-nonsense mine foreman who hadn't had much input so far.

"If, God forbid, we had a mine accident, what would your part be?"

Mac thought this was the most important question he'd been asked.

"As part of the community, it would be my responsibility to learn and prepare ahead of time for any disaster. The church should be an emergency center, and my job would be to give aid and comfort to the families during their ordeal," he replied.

The miner nodded his head in approval.

"Are you a gardener, Reverend Arnett?"

The question came from the fifth and last member of the committee, Mrs. Cornwallis. Mac had pegged her as a woman who worried a lot. Her hands never seemed to be still.

"I ask because I'm in charge of altar flowers and the

church garden," Mrs. Cornwallis said, smoothing the flower-patterned skirt of her dress. "I wonder what suggestions you might have about our spring planting."

"Really, Beth, I don't think we can expect Reverend Arnett to have ideas about that," Mrs. Hodges said in a kind voice.

"That's okay. I'll be glad to answer the question," Mac said. "I'm sure you know a great deal more than I do about the best flowers to plant, Mrs. Cornwallis, but I would like to see a portion of the space used to grow vegetables for the less fortunate. I'd also encourage all the gardeners among you to donate excess produce to those who need it."

He looked across the long table in the church basement and met the eyes of all the committee members. Had the interview gone well? It was hard to tell. He'd quelled his initial nervousness with silent prayer and tried to answer every question as honestly as possible. One thing was sure: he would be very happy when it was over.

"We very much appreciate your time," Mrs. Hodges said in a voice that indicated the interview was done. "I'm sure all of us will pray about our decision. We'll let you know as soon as possible."

He thanked them all for the opportunity and went up the stairs feeling like a kid who'd just been let out of school. He'd done well enough on most of their questions, but if they wanted a married minister who would spend the rest of his career there, he didn't qualify. Maybe someday he would want to settle down and raise a family, but for now he wanted to be free to follow his calling wherever the Lord sent him.

Outside in the parking area, he took a minute to study the small hillside church. It was unpretentious, a tan brick structure that could have housed any small business. Only the large cross on the roof gave away its true purpose as a place of worship. When all the trees bloomed, the church would blend into its surroundings in a pleasant and fitting way.

Was this where God wanted him to continue his ministry? He had doubts about whether he could meet the congregation's expectations, but he'd learned early in his ministry that the Lord did indeed work in mysterious ways. If called, he would serve here. If not, then the Lord must have something else for him to do.

Jenny wasn't usually a clock-watcher, but she was restless and eager to leave work after cutting the stranger's hair. There was a sameness about her job that had only recently begun to trouble her. She wanted to be in a position to help people, to have some impact on their lives, not that she didn't take pride in making her clients look better. It gave them greater self-confidence, which was certainly a worthwhile goal, but was it enough to fulfill her own need to be of use to others?

She couldn't seem to get Mac out of her mind, but then, she didn't get many strangers in her chair. Generally speaking, only small boys came to Charlene's. It was a rite of passage to go to the barbershop for the first time.

She was walking home to the small ranch-style house she shared with her mother, her sister Sandy and Sandy's nine-month-old son, Toby, born after his father's desertion, when she remembered their plans for the evening. Once a month the three of them went out for dinner, a ritual that had started when her father first walked out on them. At the time Sandy had been in ninth grade and Jenny in seventh grade. They'd shared in their mother's humiliation at being abandoned, but it had been important to show the community that they were still a close-knit family. Even though it had meant saving every penny to afford it, their trips to restaurants had boosted their morale.

Back then they'd had to settle for eating inside the town's most popular fast-food place. Now that all three of them had jobs, they usually treated themselves to a nice meal at Calhoun's, a family restaurant with good home-cooked food.

Jenny hurried to shower and change before the others got home. Her mom, Gloria, worked at the town's only clothing boutique for women, a job she had even before her husband left her. Sandy worked the day shift at the pharmacy while she took college courses online, hoping someday to be an elementary school teacher.

When she was younger, Jenny had very much wanted to be a nurse, but there hadn't been any money for the neces-sary training. Maybe she'd given up too easily, but when she was offered a chance to train as a beautician, she'd accepted. Her aunt in Charleston owned a small hair salon, and she'd offered to help Jenny go to beauty school. Jenny lived with her while she learned how to be a hair stylist, and Charlene had been quick to offer her a job when she finished.

Jenny didn't regret her choice of occupation. It gave her an opportunity to work with people and bring some small measure of happiness into their lives, but part of her still wondered whether she would have made a good nurse. Lately she'd thought a lot about changing her life in some meaningful way, but it would be exceedingly hard to break the close ties to her family and leave Pleasantville.

"We're home," Sandy called out as Jenny dressed in her room. "Toby was a star in day care today. He took a three-hour nap. Are you through in the shower?"

"All done." Jenny stuck her head out of the door of her bedroom to greet her family. "Hi, Mom. How was your day?"

"Exhausting. We got in our prom dresses. Seems like the girls start shopping for them earlier every year," her mom replied.

"It's a big deal for some girls," Jenny said, not wanting to think about her senior prom and what happened afterward. Jack had picked that special evening to break her heart and tell her he was leaving. "I'll be ready in a few minutes."

Jenny enjoyed their restaurant outings, but she couldn't seem to shake a vague dissatisfaction with the way her life was going. Somehow she felt that she was meant to do more than she was now. She'd prayed about it, but so far she couldn't see a clear path.

For now, though, she resisted her mother and sister's urgings to date more and establish a long-term relationship. They, of all people, should understand why she didn't want to risk more disappointment. They'd both endured a lot of pain when the men they loved proved unfaithful. Jenny was determined not to let her happiness depend on any man.

The evening was cool but pleasant, so they decided to walk the four blocks to the restaurant after they left her sister's son with a friend who lived in the neighborhood. Toby definitely wasn't restaurant-friendly yet, and evening tended to be his crabby time.

Her sister talked nonstop, excited about the A grade she'd received in her latest online class.

"If I'd known learning things was so much fun, I would've started a long time ago. You really should look into taking some courses yourself, Jenny."

"Maybe someday," she vaguely agreed.

"You've been quiet since I got home, Jenny," her mother said. "Is there something on your mind?"

"No, I guess I got talked out at work."

She wasn't being entirely truthful. She was still wondering what Mac had been doing in town and why he'd urgently needed a haircut. But she knew better than to speculate about any man with her family. They tended to get too excited if she even mentioned a man's name. They persisted in the idea that it wasn't too late for her in the relationship department, even though she told them again and again that there was no one in Pleasantville who even mildly interested her.

Mac felt drained after his lengthy interview, but he felt it had gone well. Rather than drive the curvy, hilly route to his parents' home in Morgantown in the dark, he'd opted to spend the night in one of a cluster of cabins that served as the town's only motel and leave early in the morning. He hadn't bothered to eat since breakfast, so he was more than ready for a good dinner. The motel owner recommended a place called Calhoun's, a family restaurant, and Mac walked the six blocks or so because his physical therapist had stressed how important it was to get mild exercise for his ankle every day.

To his surprise, the unpretentious restaurant was crowded, and a number of people were waiting for a table.

"I didn't expect a crowd on a weeknight," Mac said conversationally to one of the people in line.

"Fish fry night," the elderly man said. "Best deal in town for seniors."

Mac elected to wait, even though it looked like most of the diners at the tables had just been served or were waiting for their food. He looked around the crowded room and saw one familiar face.

Smiling to himself, he walked over to the table where Jenny, the beautician who'd saved his day, was sitting with two other women.

"Hello, Jenny," he said, feeling a bit like an intruder but drawn to her table because it was nice to see a familiar face. "I wanted to thank you again for the emergency haircut. It was a lifesaver for me."

She looked surprised but quickly smiled up at him. "I was glad to help."

"I'm Jenny's mother, Gloria Kincaid. If you're here alone, we have an extra chair. We haven't ordered yet," the older woman said.

Mac demurred but was easily persuaded when the third woman introduced herself as Jenny's sister, Sandy, and repeated the invitation.

"If you're sure you don't mind." He looked at Jenny for approval, and she nodded slightly. "I'm Mac, Mac Arnett."

She was prettier than he remembered. Her honey-blond hair fell in waves around her face, and her flawless complexion was tinged with pink. He hoped she wasn't blushing because he was making her uncomfortable. She kept her eyes averted, studying the menu as though she'd never seen it before.

"What brings you to our town, Mr. Arnett?" Gloria asked, her tone friendly but her eyes avid for information.

"Mother." Jenny quietly rebuked her.

"Please, call me Mac." He glanced at Jenny, wondering whether she was shy or just embarrassed by her mother's curiosity. "Actually, I had a job interview."

"Really? Was it with the town council? I heard they need an accountant in the tax office," Sandy said.

"Afraid I'm not qualified for that. I interviewed at the Bible Church."

"You're going to be our new minister?" There was respect in Gloria's voice.

"I haven't received a call yet," he was quick to point out.

He looked at Jenny to see her reaction, but she looked down at the menu again. Some women shied away from clergymen. Others tried to put them on a pedestal. Jenny gave nothing away about the way she felt.

"I can't imagine that you wouldn't," her mother said. "It's so hard for a church in such a small town to find a minister. Reverend Dulles was here forever. It was a great loss when he had to retire for health reasons."

"He was seventy-two," Jenny reminded her mother. "He deserved some leisure time."

Mac agreed with her, but the waitress came to the table so he didn't need to second her opinion. They all ordered the fish special, which came with hush puppies, cabbage slaw and hot rolls served family style.

"Where have you been working?" Sandy asked.

He explained his work as a missionary and the injury that had brought him back to the States. Jenny's mother and sister asked good questions, but Jenny herself didn't join in their conversation. He tried not to stare at her, but his eyes were pulled to her again and again.

They were just running out of small talk when their food came. There was enough breaded and deep-fat fried fish on his plate to feed a whole family in Guatemala, but he had to stop thinking like a missionary and focus his attention on ways to help people in need wherever he found them.

He was more interested in talking to Jenny than in eating, but she only made an occasional comment, letting her mother and sister dominate the conversation. He wasn't able to draw Jenny into it, hard as he tried. When she did speak, her voice was soft and pleasant. Was she unhappy because he'd joined them? He hoped not.

"You've been a lot of places for someone who grew up in West Virginia," Jenny commented after he told them about his latest mission.

"I've always loved seeing new places and meeting new people," he said. "Have you always lived in Pleasantville?"

"Oh, yes, we're born and bred right here," her mother said, answering for her.

This was his chance to learn more about the church from three of its members, but he was more interested in learning about Jenny and her situation. He gathered that she was single and lived with her mother and sister, but she seemed content to let the conversation swirl around her without taking an active part.

He ate with a good appetite, but he always enjoyed a meal in congenial company. Jenny was a dainty eater, not picking at her food but quietly savoring small bites. Was she self-conscious because of him? Ministers had that effect on some people, but he hoped she wasn't ill at ease because he was there. He found himself talking too much in his effort to find out more about her.

"Oh dear," Gloria said. "I almost forgot. I promised my friend Judy I'd stop by this evening. She has a book I've been wanting to read."

"I'll walk you part way, Mom," Sandy offered. "I trade babysitting time with a friend," she explained to Mac, "but I don't want to take advantage of her. Anyway, I'm kind of eager to spend some time with my little guy before he goes to bed."

"No need to rush through your dinner, Jenny. She always was a slow eater," her mother said for Mac's benefit.

"Well, it was awfully nice meeting you, Reverend," Sandy said as she stood to leave.

"You are all right with walking home alone, aren't you?" Gloria asked Jenny.

"I'd be happy to see you to your door," Mac quickly offered.

"I couldn't put you to the trouble," Jenny said.

"No trouble at all. I like a walk after dinner," he assured her.

Jenny knew what her mother was up to. She was deliberately throwing her at the minister. Would she never give up playing matchmaker?

Sandy gathered up the Styrofoam containers with their leftovers and gave Mac a big smile. She was shorter and had darker hair than her sister, but Jenny always thought of her as the pretty one in the family. In spite of her own terrible experience with her ex-husband, she was forever urging Jenny to go out more and date some of the eligible men in town.

Like mother, like daughter, Jenny thought with resignation. But the truth was that Mac was different from the men she knew. She welcomed a chance to talk to him alone and learn what kind of man the church committee was considering as their minister.

"I guess we should relinquish our table," he said when her mother and sister had left. "There's still quite a line."

"Yes, I forgot about fish fry night when we came. Calhoun's usually isn't busy on weeknights."

When they were out on the pavement in front of the restaurant, she realized for the first time that she had to look up to him. At five feet ten, she was eye-to-eye with most of the men she knew. Mac had to be at least four inches taller. With his face clean shaven and his hair neatly trimmed, he looked like a different person from the stranger who'd come into the shop. He was wearing a navy pullover sweater with the collar of his white shirt showing against the tan of his face, a ruddy hue that he must have acquired on his last mission assignment. His eyes were a vibrant blue that contrasted with his dark brown hair.

"You'll have to show me the way to your place," he said in a low, mellow voice that lacked the West Virginia accent that was familiar to her.

"Yes, of course." She realized that she'd been standing there like a mannequin, not quite sure what she thought about a man who was so different from all the others she knew.

She started walking briskly toward the side street that led to home.

"I hate to ask, but could we walk a little slower?" he said, sounding reluctant to mention it. "I had major surgery on my ankle, and it's still not a hundred percent."

"Oh, I'm sorry. You really don't need to walk me home."

"I want to," he said firmly. "I'm supposed to walk every day."

He crooked his arm, and it seemed the most natural thing in the world when she placed her hand on it.

"Do you really think you'll be coming to work here?" she asked.

"It's up to the search committee whether they want me," he said.

"And if they do, will you accept?"

"I'll have to pray and consider it," he replied.

"How will you know what God's answer is?"

It was such a thoughtful question that he stopped to consider it for a moment.

"How can I explain?" he asked, more to himself than her. "There's a feeling of relief when the decision is made. I believe in proceeding as the way opens. If there's an opportunity to serve God and help others, my heart speaks for me. I believe it's divine inspiration."

She was silent for a long moment, then she smiled with warmth and understanding.

"I think our church would be very fortunate to have you."

"Maybe," he said, grinning for reasons he didn't try to comprehend. "I'm a little unorganized sometimes, especially when I'm obsessed with a new project. And I've been known to be absentminded."

"We have a very efficient church secretary," Jenny said. "She keeps things organized."

"I met her. That's good to know."

"Anyway, that's not what the church needs. How can I explain it? It's like walking into a room with one dim table lamp. You can see everything important, like where the furniture is so you don't bump into it. Then click on overhead lights, and suddenly you see all the things you've missed before. Our church needs someone who can turn on the bright lights." She shook her head. "That's probably a silly way to put it."

"It's a wise way." He was practically speechless at her spiritual grasp.

They walked in silence for a few minutes. He was in awe of her insight, but his senses were clouded by the sweet flowery scent of her perfume and the light touch of her hand on his arm.

Mac wasn't sure how to react to her, but Jenny was the most extraordinary person he'd met in some time. Certainly she was attractive. She was tall and willowy with eyes that seemed to change color when he looked directly into them, but she was much more than the sum of her parts. He'd been impressed by her beauty when he'd first seen her, but she was much more than just a pretty woman.

He wanted to ask questions about the church and its congregation, but he wasn't sure how much he should ask of her as a member of the church. Before he could make up his mind, she let go of his arm and turned a corner.

"It's down here. I'd invite you in for coffee, but—" She shrugged. "It's a small town, and sometimes the windows seem to have eyes. It wouldn't increase your chances of getting the job if people started gossiping."

"No, I suppose not," he said, stopping when she did in front of her house.

"Thank you for walking me home. I'll pray that you receive a call to come here, if that's what you feel is right for you."

"Thank you. It's been a pleasure meeting you, Jenny. I hope to see you again."

In the dim light of dusk he couldn't tell whether she smiled. He did know that he wanted to get to know Jenny Kincaid better.

As he walked backed to his motel, he was more confused than ever about whether he belonged in a small-town ministry. Jenny had suggested that the church needed a charismatic leader, someone who could lead the congregation into a deeper understanding of what it meant to be a Christian. But was he that man?

He'd sensed that the committee had some reservations about him. Was it because he might be drawn back to overseas missionary work, or were they uncomfortable with an unmarried minister? Either way, he sensed that he didn't fit their preconceived notions of what a minister should be.

If they did decide to call him, he still leaned toward accepting. He kept seeing the dimly lit room that Jenny had used as an example. The more he thought about it, the more he welcomed the challenge. He also realized how easy it would be to get lost in her shimmering hazel eyes.

He shook his head at his own foolishness. Nothing complicated a minister's life more than getting involved with a member of his congregation. It was a no-win situation. If they were perceived as a couple, legions of matchmakers would expect them to set a date. If they didn't click, he would be the bad guy who let down one of their own. He liked Jenny, but she was strictly off-limits.

The whole idea of letting anything start with Jenny was premature. He didn't have the job. He wasn't even sure he wanted it. In fact, this might be the one and only time he was in the town of Pleasantville.

The walk back to the lonely little cabin seemed much longer than before. He admitted to himself that something was missing from his life, but it wasn't romance. It couldn't be. He had a lot of years to go before he even considered settling down.

Chapter Three

Mac looked around at the congregation gathered in the pews in front of him. What were they expecting from him? Could he live up to their expectations? He'd prayed long and hard about these questions before he accepted their call, which came quickly after his interview. Now he could only pray that his work, like seeds on fertile ground, would yield fruit for the Lord.

As he began his sermon, he tried not to see individual faces, especially not the woman's in the third row from the back. He'd spotted Jenny right away, almost as though her face were more luminous than all those around her.

He'd put her out of his mind while he struggled to make up his mind about staying in Pleasantville. He hadn't wanted to base his decision on the smile of a beautiful woman. In fact, he'd managed to convince himself that the instant attraction he'd felt for her would fade away just as quickly.

He knew he had to prove both to himself and the congregation that he was the right person to become their minister. They'd made that very clear by offering only an interim position for one year. The relief he felt in making only a one-year commitment balanced their lack of confidence in him. Their unspoken but obvious wish was for a married minister who would make the town his permanent home.

After the service, he began the serious job of learning the names of people in the congregation. They'd thoughtfully worn nametags this morning—a great help when he had so many new people to meet. He was gifted with a good memory, but this morning he had to put forth extra effort to concentrate on members' names.

The crowd slowly greeted him at the church door, but he watched for Jenny out of the corner of his eye as he shook hands. After all, it was her take on what was needed at the Bible Church that had tipped the balance in favor of accepting. When nearly everyone had stopped to welcome him, she still hadn't taken her turn.

Maybe she'd gone directly to the community room in the basement to help in the preparations for the potluck luncheon. He hoped so. Otherwise it would mean she'd left the church by the back exit, perhaps regretting what she'd said to him.

When everyone had gathered downstairs, the president of the congregation, George Darlington, gave a warm and pleasingly short welcoming speech. Everyone stood for Mac to say a blessing, and then the potluck began.

"I'm sorry your father couldn't be here," Darlington said. "I heard him preach once when we were visiting our daughter for Easter. He gives a fine sermon."

"He and my mother were sorry not to be here. He's officially retired, but he serves as a substitute wherever he's needed. This month he's down in the southern part of the state filling in for a minister who had a heart attack."

"Well, you go ahead and fill your plate, Reverend. Be sure to save room for a piece of my wife, Minnie's, chocolate applesauce cake. It won a blue ribbon at the county fair, and I guarantee it's dee-licious."

"I'll be sure to try it, and please call me Mac. Whenever I hear Reverend, I think somebody is talking to my father."

"Mac," he said laughing.

Mac had grown used to simple food on his mission assignments: mostly vegetables, rice, beans and sometimes a little chicken or fish. He didn't have an appetite for huge feasts, especially when he knew that malnutrition was a worldwide problem, even in the lush hills of West Virginia. Still, he would sample as many of the dishes as possible, knowing they'd been prepared to honor the beginning of his ministry.

He moved forward to the long serving table behind a family group, then picked up a plate and began putting a serving of salad on it. He looked down the heavily laden table and appreciated the effort that had gone into preparing all the dishes.

His plate full, he stepped forward to a separate table with hot coffee and other beverages—and looked directly into Jenny's warm hazel eyes.

"The coffee's really hot, Reverend Arnett," she warned, handing him a cup before he asked for it.

"Thank you."

He wanted to remind her to call him Mac, but for the first time since he'd left elementary school, he was tongue-tied. He'd thought a lot about what he might say when he saw her again, but his mind went blank.

"Would you like cream or sugar, or maybe artificial sweetener?"

He realized he was holding up the line. She'd asked a question to get him to move on.

"Oh, no thanks."

Embarrassed but hoping no one noticed, he picked a seat next to a woman whose name he'd temporarily forgotten. She immediately engaged him in conversation, asking about the small house he was renting because the church didn't have a parsonage.

"Yes, it's very nice. Couldn't be cleaner," he assured her, trying to divide his attention between her and the food in front of him.

When he glanced over toward Jenny, she was smiling at a cluster of small children who'd come to her table for cups of juice. Had she smiled at him when he got his coffee? He couldn't remember.

She was wearing a turquoise dress with silvery-white flowers in the pattern. His mother might choose something similar for herself, but Jenny made it look like high fashion with a scoop neck and sleeves that were little capes flowing down to her elbows.

He told himself that he was here to stay, at least for a year. There would be many opportunities to get to know Jenny, but he couldn't quell the impatience that made him eat too fast. He had the irrational feeling he wouldn't get to talk to her if he didn't act immediately. He wanted to thank her for the insight she'd given him about the job, but the worst thing a new minister could do was single out one member for special attention. This was his first church in the States, but he'd learned the job well from his father.

He remembered Mrs. Darlington's chocolate applesauce cake and excused himself to visit the dessert selection. Jenny was still manning the beverage table, but she didn't look in his direction until he stood directly in front of her to refill his cup.

"You look very nice today," he said in a soft voice that only she could hear.

He was rewarded by a small smile and a soft "Thank you."

A little boy with a chocolate mustache rushed up to the table for a juice refill. Jenny teased him about leaving all the frosting on his face and handed him a napkin, which he carried away with him.

"I liked your sermon," she said, at last speaking directly to him.

"Thank you."

"Did it take you a long time to write it?" she asked.

In truth, it had been a difficult assignment, totally different from the ones he gave at mission stations. There the needs of the people had been painfully obvious. He wasn't quite sure what the people in his new church needed to hear from him.

"Long enough, I hope," he answered her. "Have you had a chance to eat?"

"Not yet, but there's no hurry. There must be enough food left to feed another hundred people."

"I was going to get some dessert. Will you join me?"

At first he thought she was going to refuse, then she looked at the crowd. Almost everyone had finished or nearly finished their meal.

"I guess there's not much more for me to do here," she said.

The woman who'd been sitting next to him was gone, leaving a place at the table for Jenny.

"I was sitting over there," he said with a nod of his head.

"Yes, I saw. Let me get some food, and I'll join you."

She had better sense than he did. With practically the whole congregation watching everything he did, he shouldn't escort the prettiest woman in the room to his table. Gossip was born for little or no reason.

Jenny didn't know how she felt about the invitation to join the minister at his table. Her mother, sitting near the back of the large room with several of her friends, would get overly enthusiastic about it. The last thing Jenny wanted was to attract attention. She hadn't lived in a small town her whole life without learning how quickly rumors started.

She walked down the length of the food table, putting a few scoops of casserole and salad on her plate without paying much attention to what she took. She forgot to pick up a bundle of tableware wrapped in a paper napkin and had to go back.

One of her best friends, Kate Ronson, came out of the kitchen and caught up with her. Kate was a military wife who'd chosen to come back to her hometown with her little boy while her husband was overseas.

"Look at all the leftovers," Kate said. "Everyone outdid themselves for the new minister."

"Yes," Jenny agreed. "Have you eaten?"

"Enough for two people. Oh, good, you took some of my tuna casserole. We're going to be eating it for the rest of the week, and Todd doesn't like it at all."

Jenny hadn't even noticed that she'd taken a generous portion of her friend's infamous casserole. She didn't at all blame Todd, Kate's four-year-old son, for resisting it. If she hadn't been thinking about Mac instead of paying attention to what she put on her plate, she would've avoided it.

"Don't let me hold you up," Kate said. "You must be starved, waiting until the last minute to eat. I have to hurry home. My in-laws are coming this afternoon to inspect my quarters."

Kate laughed at their standing joke. Her father-in-law was a retired colonel who liked to make sure his grandson was being raised properly. Jenny knew sometimes he was a major annoyance to her friend.

Jenny looked over toward the table where Mac was still sitting. A woman in a navy striped pantsuit was sitting in the chair that had been empty and saying something to the minister. Jenny took it as a sign that she should sit somewhere else, but before she could locate another place, the woman got up and walked away.

Mac looked in her direction and nodded at the vacant chair. Jenny met his gaze and moved slowly toward him.

"Jenny, won't you join us?" he asked for the benefit of the Hawkins family, who occupied the places across from him.

"Thank you," she said automatically.

He stood, took her plate, set it on the table and pulled out the chair for her, courtesies that were sure to be noticed by anyone who was paying attention.

"Do you like that tuna stuff?" Timmy Hawkins asked her, staring at her across a dessert plate piled high with everything chocolate.

"It's good for you," Jenny said, pretty much agreeing with the ten-year-old's skeptical expression.

"You shouldn't have taken so many sweet things," his mother said. "I think we should get some plastic wrap in the kitchen and take home what's left on your plate. I don't want you getting a stomachache."

All six members of the Hawkins family said a noisy goodbye to Mac, then Jenny was alone with him at the table.

"Do you like that tuna stuff?" Mac teased.

"The crumb topping looked nice. I didn't notice the tuna," she admitted.

"It was the worst thing my mother ever served," Mac said. "She made it whenever my dad wasn't home for dinner. Worse, she threw in whatever leftover vegetables she had in the fridge. It put me off tuna, and mushy asparagus, for life."

Jenny laughed along with him, relieved that his good humor had chased away the awkwardness she'd felt about joining him.

There was nothing cozy about eating beside him.

She sampled the casserole—out of loyalty to Kate—and picked away at a green salad, while he stood beside her saying a few words to people who came up to him before they left. The kitchen helpers had started clearing tables before he had a chance to sit beside her and talk.

"So how is the tuna casserole?" he asked with a grin.

"My friend made it."

"Ah, everyone should have a good friend like you." He said it in a way that made her cheeks feel warm.

"You've made a good impression on everyone I've talked to," she told him.

"That's nice to hear. Your mother seems to be having a good time."

"She loves people. Crowds make her happy." Jenny hadn't given it much thought before, but it was true. "My sister, too. She was sorry she couldn't be here. Toby, her little boy, has a bad cold."

"That's a shame. Tell her for me that I hope he's better soon."

"Thank you. I will."

"And you?" he asked. "Would you rather be part of a large gathering or be with one friend at a time?"

Was she so transparent that he could tell she was shy in crowds? She looked up and met his intense gaze.

"I guess it depends on the circumstances," she said, not willing to admit that crowds made her uneasy.

Mac picked up on her hesitation and was sorry he'd asked. He was interested in everything there was to know about Jenny as a member of his new congregation, and he'd let curiosity get the best of him. He groped for a neutral topic that would make her more comfortable, but she spoke before he had a chance to say anything.

"It's a shame your parents couldn't be here. I'm sure they would have been very proud of you."

He smiled, reminded again of how fast news traveled in a small-town congregation.

"Mom will be glad to have me in this country for a while," he said.

"Do you think you'll be leaving when your year is up?" Her concern mirrored that of the search committee. They'd brought it up again when offering him the one-year position.

"I guess it depends on how well I fit here. I may stay until I have a long gray beard. I don't pretend to have a gift for seeing the future."

"You looked good with a beard. I was sorry to see you'd shaved it," she said with a half smile.

It was the first really personal thing she'd said to him. He felt gratified that she might see him as a man, not just as a minister.

"Maybe I'll grow it back someday when people are used to me," he said with a small chuckle.

Women were pulling off the paper coverings on the empty tables and washing the tops. Over near the door, a couple of men were starting to fold up the legs and store the portable tables while small knots of people were talking, seemingly in no hurry to leave the pleasant gathering. Mac was with them. He didn't want the event to end, especially because he found it so pleasant to talk to Jenny.

"I appreciated what you told me about the church needing a bright light. I don't know if I'm the person to fulfill that need, but you gave me a lot to think about."

She looked surprised. "I'm glad you didn't think I was being too dramatic."

"Not at all. It was a good take on leadership. I'd appreciate anything you can tell me about the needs of the congregation."

"You want me to be your secret agent?" she teased. "I don't think I'd make a good spy."

"Nothing like that," he said laughing. "I just thought it might be helpful to talk to someone who's been here a long time."

"All my life, actually. Sometimes it seems like I've been here forever. You don't know what a pleasant novelty it is to have a new voice in the pulpit. People are really excited. Everything I heard was very complimentary."

"I wasn't fishing for compliments, but thank you. A little encouragement goes a long way."

"I guess I should help clean up," she said, starting to stand.

"You haven't finished eating."

She looked down at her plate and looked surprised that there was still a good bit of food on it.

"I shouldn't have taken so much," she said. "Seeing all those plates and bowls of food, I overestimated my appetite."

"I know the feeling," he said standing up beside her. "Thank you for joining me."

"My pleasure."

Was it really a pleasure for her, or was she just saying the conventional thing? He wished he knew.

"Maybe some time we can get together just to talk— you know, without food," he said.

He was thirty years old and felt like an awkward teenager. Would she think he was asking her out socially? That wasn't the best move he could make his first week on the job, but he did enjoy talking to her.

To his immense relief, she smiled.

"I'm afraid you'd find my conversation pretty dull. I've never done anything the least bit adventurous compared to you. The farthest I've been from home was a beautician's conference in Florida, and that was only once."

Did his job as minister intimidate her? He wished he knew more about her. He had a feeling that she would make a very good friend to anyone she liked and trusted. Every instinct he had told him that she was as beautiful inside as she was to his eyes.

"You didn't say no?" he asked hopefully.

"No, I didn't say no." She gathered up their plates and started walking toward the kitchen.

She hadn't said yes either.

He looked around at the diminishing crowd and saw several people he hadn't spoken with. He knew that a friendly first contact could be critically important when a member of the congregation was in distress and needed pastoral help. He was still very much a stranger, and his missionary experience could be intimidating to people who'd never gone much beyond their own town.

Regardless of how long he stayed, he wanted to spread God's love among the congregation and beyond.

And he wanted to hear Jenny say yes.

Chapter Four

Mac dressed in a black turtleneck and his least ragged jeans Wednesday morning, making a mental note that he had to upgrade his wardrobe for the new job. T-shirts and cargo shorts weren't going to cut it.

He caught a glimpse of himself in the bathroom mirror, the only mirror in his small house, and hardly recognized himself. His tropical tan was fading, and he hadn't been beardless since the seminary. Who was this new person, and did he really belong in Pleasantville, West Virginia? Could he live up to expectations as minister of the Bible Church?

After walking up the hill, he was a bit surprised to see the aging blue Buick that belonged to the church secretary parked in her reserved spot this early in the morning. Betty Jo Dailey only worked part-time, but the church was far more to her than just a job. Mac didn't know how he would've gotten through his first week without her help. She'd kept him on track and filled him in on all the needs of the congregation, making sure he avoided pitfalls and blunders until he got used to the workings of the church.

Before going to his office, he went into the church and

sat in a pew, taking the opportunity to pray for guidance in leading the congregation.

His father had always been his mentor and role model, inspiring him to go into the ministry, but he didn't have any illusions about his own strengths and weaknesses. He was good in a crisis and wholly committed to helping those least able to help themselves, but being in charge of the day-to-day running of a church was new and a little intimidating, all the more so because he only had a one-year appointment. He was on trial, and he didn't know for sure that this was where he belonged.

One thing he had learned: he couldn't stay gloomy around Betty Jo Dailey.

"Good morning, Reverend Arnett," she trilled as he walked into the office. "Isn't this a glorious morning? A gift from the Lord if I ever saw one!"

"Good morning, Betty Jo—and remember, I told you to call me Mac. Otherwise I might think you're talking to my father."

"Oh, I'm not sure I feel right about that. I mean, you are the minister."

"But you have seniority," he said with a smile. "What's up today?"

He was still smiling to himself as she brought out the appointment calendar. If a modern-day Norman Rockwell needed a model for a grandmother, Betty Jo would have to be first choice. She was pleasingly plump with tightly curled white hair, pink cheeks and a tiny mouth that always seemed to be smiling. A widow of many years, she had a married daughter and a grandson she doted on, but the church was the focus of her life. When she wasn't doing her paid job as secretary, she was busy with other church activities.

"You have an appointment at eleven. I think she wants to talk to you about getting a divorce. Her husband drinks, and he's been known to get mean with her."

"Anything else?"

Mac didn't want to encourage Betty Jo's gossip. If she had one failing, it was the need to know everyone's business. He had to think of a way to convince her that everything she learned here was strictly confidential.

"The youth group meets tonight at seven. Wednesday is always church night, you know. The ladies' sewing circle is meeting here too because they have to assemble the newborn kits to be sent to mission headquarters. I'm sure they would like it if you look in on them."

"Yes, I can do that after the youth meeting."

"All the kids have to turn in their permission slips tonight," Betty Jo said.

"Permission for what?"

"Saturday. They're going to Nelson's Horse Farm for free lessons. I expect you'll be going too."

"Sounds like fun. Who are the sponsors?" he asked.

"Carl and Doreen Nelson have been doing it for a long time, but they're giving up the job after this week. That's why the kids get to go to their farm. Jenny Kincaid has been working with them for a couple of years, and she'll be taking over, at least temporarily. I don't think she's totally convinced that she can handle it alone, but we're trying to find someone to share the responsibility. She's really good with the younger teens. Not everyone remembers how it feels to be at that awkward age."

Jenny Kincaid. Mac smiled inside.

"Oh, I found something that might be helpful to you," Betty Jo said, pulling out a slim booklet. "It's a church directory. We had that deal a few years ago where a photographer comes and takes everyone's picture, then the church gets free directories. Ours is a bit outdated, but I thought it might help you get to know everyone by name."

"That will be a big help. Thanks, Betty Jo. I'm going to work at my desk until it's time for the appointment."

He went through the door to his inner office and closed it behind him, taking the directory with him. It was his intention to start researching his sermon for Sunday, but the clutter on his desk put him off. Somehow he'd managed to accumulate a sea of paper during his first week on the job. Most could be thrown away, he supposed, but not until he sorted through it. He sat and stared at it, remembering how much he disliked paperwork.

Mac added the church directory to one of the smaller piles, then changed his mind. It really would be helpful to go through it. He intended to make a personal call on every member, but that would take time. Meanwhile, he flipped through the pages, seeing many familiar faces but also a number he couldn't recall. He didn't try to memorize all the names in the directory, but he would make a point of looking up people before he made home visits. He stopped on the page that began with K and noticed a familiar face: Jenny Kincaid. She was in a group picture with her smiling mother and sister, but Jenny's expression was guarded, not a scowl but not a happy look either. He found himself wanting to know what was behind the wistful face in the photograph.

Quickly he closed the directory and tossed it aside. He could be interested in Jenny, very interested, but this wasn't the time or the place. He'd made the mistake of trying to have a relationship with Elizabeth, an aid worker in Africa, but their careers had made it impossible, taking them to different parts of the world before they really knew how they felt about each other. This job could very well be temporary, and allowing any woman into his life would only lead to complications.

He swept aside enough papers to make working space and located his well-worn Bible, opening it to the passage he intended to use as the theme of his sermon.

Jenny knew she should hurry home, but her feet seemed to drag of their own accord. The youth group met tonight, and much as she loved working with young people, she was more than a little nervous. This would be the Nelsons' last meeting, and so far no one had volunteered to help her take over the group. She wasn't at all sure she could handle the ambitious program by herself.

She couldn't blame the Nelsons for resigning. They'd been doing it for as long as she could remember, continuing even after their youngest son graduated from high school. Under their leadership, almost every eligible young teen in the church participated in the group's activities. Nervous as Jenny was about trying to fill their shoes, she wouldn't dream of resigning. The youth group had helped fill the emptiness in her life after her father deserted the family. Without it, she would have floundered much worse than she had.

Maybe the new minister would help until someone else agreed to be her co-chair. She found that prospect more unsettling than comforting. Sure, he was friendly, outgoing and likeable. There was no reason to feel edgy in his presence, but she did.

Mac Arnett and horses. No wonder she felt skittish. She would rather ride the wildest roller coaster than get on the back of one of those four-legged creatures. She'd gone to the horse farm for the first time last year, finally running out of excuses not to chaperone the annual trip. She'd tried to wiggle out of getting on a horse, not for a moment believing that the scary beast was docile. But, of course, with all the young kids watching, she'd had to give it a try.

She still cringed at the memory. The horse first refused to move, then stubbornly went where it pleased, totally indifferent to her frantic tugs on the reins. The ultimate humiliation came when Doreen Nelson had to walk out and lead her back. Her legs had been trembling so much that she could hardly stand when she finally slid off the saddle.

This year everyone would find out what a coward she was around horses. She shook her head, determined to watch the group from a distance, a safe distance.

"Jenny, am I glad you're home," Sandy called out as soon as she walked through the door. "Can you possibly watch Toby tonight? Mom is going to one of her clubs."

Jenny was surprised to see her sister with big foam curlers in her hair and her face smeared with pink cream.

"Where are you going?"

"Oh, you know, just out with a friend. You can babysit, can't you?"

"Sorry, it's Wednesday. Youth group night."

"Oh, I forgot. Do you have to go?"

"You know I do." Jenny wondered about her sister's urgency.

"I don't suppose—"

"No, I really can't take Toby with me," Jenny said, anticipating her sister's thought.

"I guess not. I'll just have to call Megan. I already owe her three nights of babysitting, and with her two boys, it's hard labor."

Sandy went off to her room muttering to herself, and

Jenny scooped Toby out of his playpen. His diaper had sprung a leak, and his little shirt was damp where he'd drooled. It wasn't like Sandy not to keep him dry and clean, which made her urgency even more puzzling.

Jenny nuzzled her nephew's baby-soft head, loving the tickle of his fine dark hair on her chin. In truth, she would love to spend the evening with Toby. She adored him and cherished the time spent alone with him, but she didn't let her sister and mother know this. They were far too eager to marry her off without letting them see how much she adored babies.

She grimaced, wondering why they both kept pressuring her to date. Men had caused so much trouble in their lives. Why did they want her to go through the same kind of misery? She didn't share their optimism. There was no Prince Charming waiting to carry her away to his castle. Fairy tales were for children, and she wasn't going to subject herself to disappointment, abandonment and unhappiness just because her family thought she should find someone special. It wasn't going to happen.

People were already milling around in the basement meeting room when Jenny got there. She'd helped the young people paint their meeting room last year, managing not to cringe when they covered two walls with vivid yellow and the other two with electric blue. A church member had donated secondhand rusty orange carpeting, and the old couches and chairs were covered with remnants of heavy velvet drapes that had once hung in Mrs. Hodges's stately Victorian parlor. The whole room was a hodgepodge of conflicting colors, but the kids had made it their own by filling several large corkboards with pictures of their activities.

Cindy Berry, the newly elected president of the group, was busy making checks in a notebook, counting to see if everyone was there. She swished her long blond hair whenever she went up to a cluster of boys, but she came on too strong to be popular with them.

It fascinated Jenny to watch the kids' social behavior. She identified with Emily, the shyest girl in the group, and made a special point of giving her attention. She knew how much effort it must take to keep coming when she didn't have any close friends there. Emily wasn't a pretty girl. Her short dark hair was ragged, possibly because she cut it herself, and she was painfully thin with an elfish, heart-shaped face. But Jenny suspected that she would blossom into an exotic beauty someday.

Most of the group was clustered around the Nelsons. Carl was a tall, extremely thin man full of nervous energy. He didn't say much, but when he did, the young people listened intently. His wife, Doreen, was a full head shorter and much more laid-back. She loved to talk, but she was a good listener too. Jenny was going to miss working with them, all the more so because it meant she would have full responsibility for the youth group.

She was talking to Emily, her back to the door, when she suddenly sensed a change in the room. The excited babble ceased, and she felt a shiver of anticipation. The new minister was here.

Mac quietly but efficiently worked his way around the room, greeting people he recognized and learning the names of those he hadn't met before. He kidded and joked with the young people, exactly the right way to gain their respect and affection. Jenny almost envied him for his easygoing manner and charisma, but she was grateful for it too. Their retired minister was a good man, but he had been too stiff and formal with young people, sometimes giving the impression that he was uncomfortable with them. Mac was exactly the opposite, and she could tell that they were warming to him already.

"Jenny, nice to see you."

He nodded at her then quickly focused his attention on Emily, perhaps instinctively knowing that the girl was ill at ease. With only a few words and a broad smile, he had her giggling, her awkwardness put aside.

"Okay, everybody," Doreen Nelson called out. "Let's all take a seat so we can go over the plans for Saturday."

"Yes, everyone sit down now," Cindy said in an assertive voice, not wanting anyone to forget that she was the president. "I'll collect the permission slips. If you didn't bring one, you'll have to get it to me before Saturday or you can't go."

Mac looked in Jenny's direction and smiled broadly, not mocking Cindy's officiousness but showing her that he enjoyed being there.

Jenny let her mind wander while the Nelsons went through the details of the trip to their farm. They'd kindly volunteered to grill hot dogs and hamburgers for lunch after everyone had a turn to ride, but they asked for volunteers to bring cookies and munchies. If the event was anything like last year's, it would be late afternoon before they headed home.

Was Mac going to be one of the chaperones? When he volunteered to drive, it appeared that he would be. The Nelsons were obviously pleased to have him. It was a big undertaking to keep fifteen kids entertained and out of trouble. No doubt he'd be a big help, so why did the prospect make her uncomfortable?

He was sitting across the room from her, and she carefully avoided staring at him. But whenever she glanced his way, she was struck again by how handsome he was. He had the rugged good looks that women loved: high cheekbones, strong chin, straight nose and full lips. She remembered him with dark brown hair flowing down to his shoulders and an untamed beard, but he was just as handsome with clean-shaven cheeks and a businessman's haircut. He didn't need clerical garb to be a commanding presence in the room.

"Jenny, does that work for you?"

Doreen had asked her a question, but her mind had been miles away.

"I didn't…" She hated to admit that she hadn't been paying attention.

"Is there anyone here who can't meet at the church at 8:00 a.m.?" Mac quickly asked, saving her from the embarrassment of admitting she hadn't been listening.

No one objected to the time, and she flashed him a look of gratitude. But how did he know she'd been distracted? Worse, did he realize that he was the reason she hadn't been concentrating on plans for the outing?

She risked a quick glance in his direction, and he smiled directly at her.

Busted, she thought. Somehow he knew that she'd been thinking about him, but it wouldn't happen again. It was a novelty to have a handsome new man in town, but she didn't for one minute believe that he would stay beyond his one-year appointment. He was too worldly for life in a small West Virginia town, and she knew more than she wanted to know about men who wandered in and out of women's lives.

Once she got through the outing on the farm, her life could go back on its usual tranquil path. The big question was: Which was more dangerous, the horse or the man?

Chapter Five

The road twisted and curved, taking Jenny and her three passengers steadily uphill. She was used to the narrow back roads in her home state, but the beauty of the countryside still had the power to enchant her. It was especially lovely today, the late April budding giving a fresh green cast to the heavily wooded area.

"I've never been this way before," Emily said.

"This is the third time I've been to Nelson's farm," Julia Dugan said. "I had a birthday party there when I turned twelve. It was way cool. We had a hayride, and everyone got to ride a horse. I'd love to go there every year, but Dad said it's too expensive."

Cindy, never one to be outdone, started talking about her tenth birthday party there.

"I had a piñata, and my whole class came. Of course, that was before you moved here, Emily. Wait until you see the horses. They are so beautiful!"

Beautiful! Jenny wondered whether she was the only one who feared getting up on one of the frightening creatures. She gritted her teeth, and her hands tightened on the car steering wheel, determined not to let anyone see how apprehensive she was. But her mind wasn't totally focused on her fear of horses. She kept thinking about Mac, torn between wishing he wouldn't come and wondering why she cared.

They were the last to arrive. The others were already congregating outside the large gray barn, the sliding door open to give a view of the broad aisle between the horse stalls. Beside it was another low structure, the indoor arena, and behind that there was an outdoor ring the Nelsons used for lessons. There were fenced fields and heavily trodden riding trails as far as Jenny could see.

From the parking area she could hear country music blaring out from the barn, loud enough to drown out the excited murmurs of the kids. She took a quick count, happy that everyone in the youth group had been able to come. Two sets of parents had joined them as chaperones and chauffeurs, but the only person who really caught her attention was Mac. He looked totally at home on the horse farm in his worn jeans, scruffy boots and a straw cowboy hat. The man was a chameleon. He looked like he belonged, no matter where he was.

She, however, couldn't have felt more out of place. Her jeans and the plaid cotton shirt borrowed from her mother were okay for a farm outing, but inside she was a town girl who really didn't want to be there.

"Here they are!" Mac called out, walking to meet her group. "Carl was just about to give us a tour of the barn."

The three girls from her car ran ahead to join the others, but Mac fell into step beside her.

"Any trouble finding the place?" he asked.

"No, I was here last year."

"It's quite a setup," he said enthusiastically. "I haven't

been on a horse since the surgery on my ankle, but I can't wait to hit the trail."

"How is your ankle?" she asked, just for something to say.

"Eighty percent. At least I don't limp like a lame duck anymore," he said with a small chuckle.

He took her elbow and guided her toward the entrance to the barn. It was a casual gesture, and one the others didn't even notice in their excitement to get near the horses. Jenny felt a tremor in her arm and hoped he wouldn't suspect how nervous she was.

Doreen led them into the barn, talking nonstop and loud enough to be heard over the music.

"This is the tack room on the left. You can see that we keep saddles, bridles and such in there. We tiled the floor and installed heat a few years ago. Those are cross ties," she said pointing, "which are ropes that can clip on either side of a horse's halter if we need to restrain it for any reason."

Jenny thought the barn looked enormous, and the rows of stalls on either side seemed to go on for blocks.

"We have twenty-two stalls," Doreen went on. "Besides our own, we board an average of eight to ten horses."

All Jenny saw were horses' heads peering over the gates that kept them confined. She had to admit they were beautiful—until one opened black lips to show huge teeth. One high-spirited spotted monster was restlessly stomping the floor of its stall, and she could imagine those lethal hoofs coming down on her. She shuddered involuntarily and was surprised to feel Mac's light touch on her arm.

"Now, how many want to ride?" Doreen asked when they got to the end of the barn.

Only one of the parents raised a hand, and Jenny was

greatly tempted to beg off herself. She was shocked when Mac lifted her arm.

"The only way to get over being afraid is to meet your fear head-on," he whispered so only she could hear.

"How do you know—"

"You're trembling, and I don't think it's me you're afraid of."

She slammed her arm down by her side, but Doreen had already counted her.

"I hate horses," she protested in a whisper.

"No, you don't. They're one of the most beautiful creatures God made. Once you get over your fear, you'll love them."

She wanted to sit and watch. She did not want to get on the back of a horse.

"We'll go out in three groups. Everyone will start in the ring, but I know some of you ride well enough to go out on a trail with our son Dave. When you're not having your turn to ride, you can go in back of the barn. There are picnic tables and some play equipment, or you might like to play horseshoes. Everyone will get equal time. Now, how many feel they're experienced enough for a trail?"

Nearly half of the children and the one parent raised their hands. Carl picked the first group at random from those who claimed experience and led them off to the ring. Teddy, a weathered-looking older man who worked for him, and Dave, the Nelsons' older son, began leading out the horses.

"If you know how to ride, why didn't you raise your hand and go on the trail?" Jenny asked Mac.

"I'm not in any hurry, but some of the kids can't wait to mount up. I'll get my turn eventually."

He didn't say it, but she suspected he wanted to ride

at the same time she did. She still didn't know whether
she could force herself to get on a horse. Her mind was
frantically searching for a way to get out of it without
looking like a big sissy in front of the kids.

She was much too nervous to sit on a bench or play a
game of horseshoes, so she walked over to the wire barrier
that fenced in the learner's ring. From there she could see
the horses being led out one at a time. Part of Carl's lesson
included saddling a horse. He and Doreen showed each
person individually, then helped them mount, checking
the stirrups to make sure they were the right length. Only
when they were satisfied that a rider knew the basics did
they let him or her slowly circle the sandy track.

"They're doing well," Mac said, coming over to stand
beside her. "Look at Emily. She knows what she's doing."

"Yes." Jenny was amazed at the diminutive girl's com-
posure on the back of a huge white horse named Snow-
flake. Under her firm hand, the mammoth beast was
ambling around the ring with his rider in complete control.

Emily was the first to be picked for a trail ride. Jenny
was immensely proud of her and glad that her status in
the group would be raised by her equestrian skills.

Maybe by the time it was Jenny's turn all the big horses
would be taken. She could handle a pony, say one the size
of a Saint Bernard dog. She couldn't remember seeing
one little enough to seem safe, but surely the Nelsons
must have some for young beginners. She didn't even care
if she looked silly on a too-small mount as long as she
didn't have to climb up a mountain of hostile horseflesh.

Finally Carl was satisfied that the first group was competent enough to leave the ring for a trail ride. His son, a
carbon copy of his father except for an unwrinkled face
and the thick dark hair showing at the edges of his cowboy

hat, led the group, turning often to be sure no one was having trouble.

The second group didn't need to be summoned. They were lined up by the fence, ready and eager for their turns. Jenny expected Mac to go with them, but he still hung back, staying by her side and calling out words of encouragement to the novice riders.

The trail riders were out of sight, and Jenny prayed that none of them would come to any harm. She especially worried about Emily. Her horse was so huge! What if it decided to break into a run or tried to throw Emily off? Was she really as competent as she'd looked in the ring?

The second group took much longer to get mounted, and Doreen led them around and around the ring, calling out instructions and encouraging the riders to feel at ease. After what seemed like ages, the Nelsons agreed that they could try an easy trail that led around the farm buildings and through a field. They would stay in sight, unlike the first group. Teddy would lead them or, as it turned out, shepherd them like a flock of sheep, riding up and down the line to make sure everyone had their horse under control.

"They're doing great," Mac said, still beside her.

The day was getting warmer, and she could smell the spicy scent of aftershave. But far from allaying her fears, his kind words were making her even more nervous. She didn't want to look like a fool in front of anyone, but especially not him. Kids half her age had waltzed through their lessons, making it look easy to ride a horse, but she had a vision of her crushed body lying in the dust, trampled by massive hooves.

She thought of a dozen reasons not to step into the ring

and saddle up. All of them seemed silly as she played them through her mind.

"You can do this," Mac said in a gentle, persuasive voice. "I guarantee it."

"Guarantee it? How can you do that?"

"I have faith."

How could she argue with that? Reluctantly she opened the gate for the waiting young people, then followed them into the ring, sensing Mac right behind her.

"Here, try this one, Jenny," Doreen called out to her, holding the reins of a brown horse that towered over the short woman. "She's a mare and gentle as they come. Her name is Mudpie, but I've always said we should have given her a nicer name after we bought her."

Much to her surprise, Mac walked past her and went up to the horse's head, murmuring softly and stroking the dark face. Apparently he charmed horses as easily as people.

Jenny's feet felt weighed down, and she moved forward slower than her little nephew could crawl. Carl was giving her instructions, but his words didn't sink in. She remembered how to mount, but she couldn't seem to fit her foot in the stirrup. It kept sliding out, and she could feel heat rising to her face.

"Let me give you a boost." Mac bent beside her and offered his cupped hands.

It didn't seem right to step on the man's hands, but he didn't give her a choice. He raised her foot without any conscious effort on her part, then steadied her as she swung her other leg across the horse's back.

She was on. She wanted to get off.

Mac and Carl both looked so pleased that she felt like a colossal fraud. She clutched the saddle horn as if it were a lifeline, grateful that at least Carl had chosen a western saddle for her. Last time she'd had an English saddle, and there hadn't been any safe handhold.

Carl guided her hands onto the reins and gave her some rudimentary instructions.

Okay, she could sit here. If she fell, she'd probably only break a few bones.

But please, Lord, please, don't let this thing move.

It ambled slowly forward, and she realized that Mac, not one of the Nelsons, was leading it. She looked down at the ground and fought off a dizzy feeling while he continued to murmur to the horse. She swayed in the saddle, sure that she would plunge to her death any moment, but all that happened was a gentle rocking motion. She was riding.

"Please, horse, please, go slow," she said louder than she'd intended.

The thing had a name. Muddy…no, Mudpie. What an awful name! Was it because the horse had a habit of throwing riders into the mud? No, that couldn't be. The ring was dry sand, and there was no way she would be going out on a trail. She trusted Carl to see what an awful rider she was.

She and Mudpie circled all the way around the ring, and it only took what seemed like a few hours. Surely now she could get off without totally disgracing herself. But no, they started around again, and she was horrified to notice that Mac was no longer leading. How could he leave her up here alone?

What on earth made her think that Mac was her guardian angel? He'd only shown kindness because he sensed that she was scared. He couldn't possibly know how terrified she was.

The horse knew what it was doing even if she didn't. It started around for the third time, then again and again until she lost count. She resisted the urge to yell for help. Other horses were ambling past her now, but one pulled up so close beside her that her leg brushed against the rider's.

"Are you okay?" Mac asked in a soft voice.

"I guess."

"You're doing great."

She risked a sideward glance. He sat his horse, a lively looking brown-and-white spotted one, with the assurance of a born horseman. She realized that he'd passed up his chance to get a nice trail ride because he knew she was frightened.

She straightened in the saddle and resolved to get through this with her dignity intact even if it killed her.

Mac hid his smile with a fake yawn and let Jenny's horse get a few paces ahead of his. The Nelsons had given her a gentle nag that they only used with rank beginners. She was safer on Mudpie's back than she would be in a rocking chair on her own front porch, but no one could convince her of that. She had to learn for herself that riding was not only safe, but also fun.

"You're really doing great!" he called over to her. "Carl said I could take you out on the easy trail when you're ready."

"Maybe on my hundredth birthday," she answered with alarm.

"We'll ride over to the creek that runs through the north pasture, maybe a five-minute walk on foot. It will let the kids see that you're willing to try new things."

"A walk sounds nice—on my own two feet. You go ahead and catch up with the first group."

"Jenny, you're as safe on Mudpie's back as you would be home in your own bed."

"Oh, sure," she said skeptically. "That's why Carl makes everyone wear this hat thing."

"His insurance probably requires some kind of helmet. Your fear of horses is a phobia, not a rational fear. The Nelsons certainly wouldn't let a bunch of kids loose with their valuable animals if they weren't confident about their safety. I know exactly how you feel, only with me it's snakes. You have no idea how much they scare me, but I had to get over it to do mission work."

"How did you do it?" At least she sounded interested.

"I picked up a few, got acquainted with some nonpoisonous ones. I'm still leery of the dangerous ones, but at least there's good reason to be scared of them."

"You think if I pet a few horses, I won't be afraid of them?"

"It probably won't be that easy, but you're making a good start. Let go of the saddle horn and stroke Mudpie's neck. Trust me, she'll love it, and I won't let anything happen to you."

He heard her deep sigh and for a moment thought she wouldn't do it. Then she reached forward and petted the animal's sleek coat.

"It feels like velvet." The wonder in her voice touched something deep inside of him.

"Let's try the trail. We can turn around any time you like."

Except for a couple of beginners who were still circling the ring, they were the only ones who hadn't gone out on a trail.

"I'm not ready," she protested with a hint of panic in her voice.

"Jenny, the chance of old Mudpie galloping off and throwing you is less than being hit by a falling space satellite. And I'll be right beside you if she even hiccups."

"You'll turn around if I say so?"

"Absolutely. I promise."

"Okay." She sounded petrified but managed to guide the horse to the open gate that led to a beginners' trail across the pasture.

His heart swelled with pride at her willingness to try, even though they hardly knew each other. What he did know was that Jenny was a special person. He could read fear in her stiff back and frozen profile, but she was slowly taking control of her mount and gaining confidence.

"She's going without me doing anything," she said with surprise.

"You are doing something, giving her her head on a familiar trail. You're riding a horse, Jenny. I'm proud of you."

"Thank you," she whispered. "But I don't know how to turn around when we get to the creek."

"I'll help you," he promised again.

Belatedly it occurred to him that he was a chaperone and shouldn't be giving all his attention to Jenny. At least all the kids seemed to be having a great time, and he hated to see anyone paralyzed by fear.

She'd pulled her honey-blond hair back into a ponytail that swished in the wind as she rode, and he fell back behind her, continuing to call out encouragement.

"You're doing great, Jenny."

She took a deep breath when they reached the little bridge that crossed the creek. He wished they could continue riding, but he'd promised to turn around. He reached out for her reins, glad that Mudpie had proved so docile. Still, the big horse dwarfed her, even though she was a tall woman, and her vulnerability touched his heart.

"Can we go back now?"

"Sure."

He didn't try to persuade her to go farther on the trail, but he wondered whether he could continue thinking of her as just another member of the congregation.

Chapter Six

"There's a woman here to see you," Betty Jo said before Mac could say good morning on Tuesday.

He looked around the office and didn't see anyone, but his secretary was definitely flustered.

"I had them go to the nursery room. She had four children with her, all younger than school age. I thought they'd get in less trouble there."

"Good idea," Mac said. "I'll go see her."

"Please do," Betty Jo said, as though the weight of the world had just been lifted from her shoulders. "The poor thing has a whole lot of trouble."

Mac knew how kindhearted Betty Jo was, but this was the first time he'd seen her this disturbed. He hurried down the corridor that led to the Sunday school rooms.

"Good morning. I'm Reverend Arnett. What can I do for you?" he asked as he walked into the playroom.

One little boy was listlessly pushing a toy truck back and forth, but the other three children were clustered around a thin, pale-skinned woman with dark hair pulled back from her face.

"I didn't know where else to go," she said in a teary voice, dabbing at her eyes with a crumpled up tissue.

Mac pulled up a kid-size chair and sat down in front of her. "Why don't you start at the beginning and tell me what's troubling you?"

"My husband…" She started sobbing, and Mac strained to make out what she was saying.

"The cops took him to jail. Drunk and disorderly. He's on parole, so this time they'll send him away for sure. I haven't been able to work since little Jeffrey came—my back is bad—and I don't know what will become of us."

"Let's take it a step at a time," Mac said.

He looked around for a box of tissues and found one on top of a supply cupboard. After he handed it to the woman, he sat down in front of her again.

"First, tell me your name."

"Lillian Smithson." She blotted her eyes and made an obvious effort to control her emotion. "I went to Social Services, but they gave me all these papers to fill out." She pulled a wad of folded sheets from the canvas bag that served as her purse. "The food pantry can't help until I get on their list. And I can't get on their list until I fill out the papers. But you see, Reverend—" She cried even harder now. "I never did learn much reading. My pa wasn't one to stay in one place."

"We can help you with that," Mac said in a soothing voice.

"My little ones are hungry now. I fed them the last I had, but they ain't had supper last night nor breakfast either."

Mac ran the options through his head, trying to remember what his father did in situations like this. One thing a minister shouldn't do was hand out money. Unfortunately, the church couldn't set a precedent for giving out cash without becoming vulnerable to more requests than they could possibly handle. But this family needed immediate help.

"Tell you what," he said. "I'll get Betty Jo to help you with the papers, and I'll see about getting some groceries to tide you over."

Her thanks were as tearful as her appeal for help, but Mac finally managed to bring Betty Jo down to handle the papers while the children shyly investigated the toys in the room.

He knew the church had a contingency fund for emergencies, but he hadn't realized how strapped it was. He found a total of fourteen dollars and fifty cents tucked away in a small metal safe and decided he would need to buy some groceries with his own money.

An hour later, Lillian and her children were on their way home with several bags of nourishing food, hopefully enough to last until her first relief check. Mac delivered her paperwork himself, wanting to be sure there were no delays.

"Do many people come here for help?" he asked Betty Jo after he returned and before going into his office to tackle the growing pile of work on his desk.

"Not a lot, but we seem to be getting more since the economy is so bad. We used to have our own food pantry, but folks sort of forgot about it when the town opened one."

"Apparently there are people who fall through the cracks," he said thoughtfully.

This was something he wanted to consider seriously, and he knew just the person to discuss it with him.

Jenny knew her mind wasn't on her job this week. Mrs. McShane's perm turned out a little frizzy, and Minnie Darlington hadn't seemed at all pleased by her cut.

Maybe it was time for a drastic change in her life, but she felt at loose ends, unable to make decisions.

Face it, she told herself, everything seemed out of kilter since the outing at the farm. She couldn't stop thinking about Mac's kindness, nor could she forget how he'd helped with her phobia about horses. He'd picked up on her nervousness and helped her work through it without causing fuss or embarrassment.

Jenny wanted to thank him, but she didn't want him to think she was flirting with him. She was just a member of his congregation. Even if she wanted to be more than that to him—and she emphatically did not—it would be a very bad idea. A new minister had the whole church watching everything he did. She didn't need or want this kind of scrutiny, especially not from her matchmaking mother and sister. She felt so strongly about this that she'd hurried away after the Sunday service without even a church-door greeting.

She wandered up to the desk and checked the appointment book, glad to see that one of her good friends was next on the schedule. Kayla Burns had been an adversary in grade school, but in middle school they'd discovered how much they liked the same things. Their friendship had blossomed and lasted until the present. Now the biggest thing they had in common was their unmarried state. Most of their former classmates had husbands and children, so the two of them often did things together.

"I want you to take off just a teeny, tiny bit," Kayla said a few minutes later when she was settled into Jenny's chair after her shampoo.

"You don't really need a cut," Jenny said, a warning she gave almost every time Kayla came in.

"Oh, I know, but the back looks so uneven. My hair seems to grow faster on the left than the right."

Jenny had her doubts about that, but a light trim always seemed to energize her friend. Kayla was petite, and her short black hair gave her an impish look. She worked at an insurance agency as receptionist, secretary and all-around organizer, but she was beginning to get restless in her job, just as Jenny was lately. Kayla had talked about leaving town for several years, but so far she hadn't made any move to do it. Like Jenny, she lived with her family, and her mother was hard-pressed to take care of her ailing husband.

"I looked for you after church," Kayla said. "You must have ducked out fast. How did the horse farm go?"

"Better than I expected, but I'd be happy never to go there again."

Jenny laughed lightly, although her heart wasn't in it.

"I'd ride a rhino at the zoo to spend the day with our new minister. Doesn't he have the most mellow voice you've ever heard?"

Kayla sounded so wistful that Jenny didn't know how to answer her. Her friend never lacked for boyfriends, but she never settled on one for very long. Either her expectations were too high, or she was just plain unlucky.

"How does he look on a horse?" Kayla asked, holding the hand mirror so she could watch as Jenny carefully trimmed the hair at the back of her neck.

"Like he belongs on one, I guess."

"I mean, what did you do there besides riding?"

"You could have come with us. I did ask you," Jenny reminded her.

"I didn't think I belonged there with all those kids." Kayla shifted restlessly under the nylon cape.

"We had some adults come too. By the way, I still

need a co-sponsor for the youth group. You wouldn't be interested, would you?"

"No, I'm not good with teenagers. They don't respect me because they can look down on the top of my head."

"Doreen Nelson is short, and she's great with kids. I wish they weren't retiring from the group, but they've led it for years and years."

"Oh, but she's old," Kayla said, as if age automatically commanded respect. "So what did Reverend Arnett wear? When I think of a minister, I think black suit."

"Ministers are just ordinary men with a calling. He looked perfectly at ease in jeans, T-shirt, hat, boots, just standard riding clothes."

"Real cowboy boots and a ten-gallon hat?"

"No, alligator boots and a clown hat," Jenny teased, wanting to change the subject.

The last thing she wanted to tell Kayla was the way Mac had helped her through the ordeal with the horse. She didn't want to arouse her friend's curiosity, so there was no point in making a big deal about his ministry or his personality.

"There, how's that?" she asked after she blow-dried Kayla's naturally curly hair. "You shouldn't need another trim for at least six weeks."

"Unless something special comes up, like a date with a new man."

Jenny felt a little morose after Kayla left. She hoped her friend didn't have a crush on the new minister, but no doubt he was going to be popular with the women in the church. At least she wouldn't be part of the adoring hoard. She didn't want her life complicated by any man. Her mother still had emotional scars from her father, although he'd died of cancer several years ago. When she let herself think about him, she still felt a deep sadness. The hurt never quite went away, and she wasn't going to risk that kind of pain again.

When Mac had an idea in his head, he couldn't wait to get started. This time, though, he had to consider the best way to enlist Jenny's help. A telephone conversation didn't seem adequate. He wanted to see her in person.

He thought of making a pastoral call on her family, remembering that his father usually dropped in unannounced so people wouldn't feel they needed to clean house or prepare refreshments. In fact, he wanted to visit all the church members eventually.

No, a call at her home seemed too contrived. He needed to talk to Jenny, and there was no reason not to call her and ask for an appointment. He knew that the youth group was important to her. Why else would she subject herself to the ordeal of riding a horse?

He ate a quick supper at a café near his rented house, then walked back to the church, glad that his ankle seemed stronger and less painful than it had just a week ago.

His day had been full of interruptions, some worthwhile and others just social visits from members of the congregation who wanted to get to know him better. There were no meetings scheduled this evening, so it was the perfect opportunity to finally clear away the paperwork on his desk. First, though, he'd call Jenny and see when they could get together to talk about his new idea.

She answered the phone herself in a reserved tone that didn't seem to change when he identified himself.

"Reverend Arnett, this is quite a surprise."

What would it take to make people in this town call him Mac?

"Do you think we could get together for a meeting sometime soon?" he asked. "It concerns the youth group."

"Have you found someone to help me?"

"Afraid not, but I'll be your backup for now. I enjoy working with kids. When do you think we can talk about some plans?"

"Evenings are best for me. My day off varies from week to week."

"How about tonight? I can come to your place if you like."

"Things get pretty hectic around here at Toby's bedtime. I could meet you at the church."

"Great, that's where I am now. Come over whenever it's convenient."

He hung up, hoping to get some paperwork done while he waited for her, but his mind kept leapfrogging back to the outing at the horse farm. Jenny always seemed so calm and self-possessed. It had been a revelation to see her vulnerable side. In fact, she'd been on his mind a lot since Saturday, even though he had no intention of getting involved with anyone during his one-year appointment. He wasn't going to mistake occasional loneliness for an urge to settle down permanently.

Maybe he should approach the outreach committee or one of the women's groups with his idea instead of putting it to Jenny first. But no, he wanted to involve the young people of the church, and that meant running the idea past their leader.

He checked the wall clock in his office every two or three minutes, finally giving up on his paperwork. He went outside and circled the church, looking at the shrubs that softened the austere lines of the building. The garden area behind the church had been plowed, and he hoped it would yield a sizable harvest of vegetables. The longer he was in town, the more he saw the needs of the less fortunate people in the area.

Worried Jenny would come and think he wasn't there, he hurried back to his office, making sure the corridor lights were on. He didn't want her to think the church was deserted.

She came less than half an hour after his phone call, but it had seemed like hours. When had he been so eager to see anyone? He couldn't remember, but he dismissed it as enthusiasm for his idea.

"Thanks for coming so quickly," he said, walking out of his office to meet her as soon as he heard the outer door close.

"No problem. You sounded excited about something."

"Actually, I am."

He wasn't sure whether to invite her into his office or ask her to join him on the bench outside the church entrance. He opted for the open air. For both their sakes, it would be better to be seen there than be surprised in his office by a member of the congregation.

"Tell me," she prompted as they sat side-by-side overlooking the empty parking area.

"I had a visitor this morning, a mother with her young children. The bottom line was that she didn't have food for her kids. She'll get relief soon, but until she works her way through the system, she can't get supplies from the town food pantry."

"We used to have a food closet at the church," Jenny said thoughtfully. "It didn't seem necessary after the town opened their pantry."

"I'm sure they do a good job with their regulars, but some people fall through the cracks, even if only temporarily."

"Even Pleasantville has some homeless, especially transients in the summer," she said.

"I'd like to reopen the church food pantry," Mac said.

"What can I do to help?"

He loved that she offered to help without any persuading. Hopefully the church council would be as agreeable as she was.

"I'm hoping the youth group will get involved. There's a large supply room between the church office and the closet with the choir robes. There's not that much in it, so I think it can be cleaned out and used as a food pantry. It will need painting and possibly more shelves."

"I'm sure the young people will be glad to help. Most of the ones who come regularly are too young to have summer jobs. This is the perfect project for them. When the room is ready, maybe they can do some fundraising, car washes or bake sales to earn money to buy groceries."

"Wonderful!" he said, delighted by her response. "Eventually we'll have to rely on donations from the congregation, but that's a great way to get started."

"Cindy, the president, can be a little officious, but she's a great organizer. I think she'd really throw herself into it."

"They all seemed like good kids," Mac said. "That's partly why I thought of them."

"Do you think the church council will approve? They don't always embrace new ideas very quickly."

"I think they can be persuaded," Mac said. "The real question is: Am I asking too much of you? Will you have time to do it?"

"I'll make time. It's a really good idea, Mac."

He took it as a good sign that she called him by his first name. He hadn't realized how much he'd wanted her support for his idea.

"As I said, I'll help you as much as I can. Maybe when people see that the youth group is more than a social club, someone will volunteer to co-sponsor it," he said.

He tried to sound serious and businesslike, but inside his heart was singing. Was it possible that the most beautiful woman in town had as much zeal for helping others as he did? He realized that he was excited to work with her on this project. But a little voice in his head was cautioning him. It would be much too easy to become seriously interested in Jenny, and that wouldn't do at all.

"One more thing," he said, feeling a bit guilty for asking because it had nothing to do with the food pantry, "I won't be intruding on your private life, will I, taking up too much of your time?"

"You mean, am I seeing anyone right now?"

She raised one eyebrow, and he wasn't sure how to interpret her look.

"Something like that," he admitted uncomfortably.

"No, there's no one special in my life, and I don't expect that there will be in the near future."

She said it so emphatically that he raised his eyebrows, unintentionally showing surprise.

"Oh." He didn't know how else to react.

"I guess that sounded harsh," she said. "I just haven't had much luck with men, starting with my father. He deserted us when I was a kid."

"That can be a hard thing to deal with," he said sympathetically.

"It was a long time ago."

"So you've never had a serious boyfriend?"

He could understand how hurt she must have been, but he couldn't believe it had soured her forever on men.

"One. He left. I really have to be going, Reverend Arnett."

He was Reverend Arnett again. She was using his name like a weather vane, showing which way the wind was blowing. It was annoying and amusing at the same time.

For now he'd have to be satisfied that she would help establish an emergency food pantry in the church, but he badly wanted to understand the undertone of bitterness in her voice when she mentioned her father and a former boyfriend. She was a charming, generous and compassionate woman, but pain had given her a hard edge that she usually concealed. Jenny puzzled him, but he wanted her friendship almost as much as he wanted to help her deal with her past.

"I should be going," she said, making him realize that there'd been several moments of silence between them. "I promised to give Toby his bath, and it's almost his bedtime."

"I'll walk you home," he offered.

"You don't need to, really. The streets are safe in Pleasantville."

"Well, thanks so much for coming and for offering to help."

He watched her walk away, a flowered skirt swishing around her knees as she moved. Her stately posture was elegant and self-assured. If he hadn't seen her vulnerable side at the horse farm and heard the pain in her voice this evening, he might think she was the most self-confident woman he'd ever met.

He smiled to himself. Jenny was an enigma. He was looking forward to working with her more than he would've believed possible when he accepted this job.

He had to remember how complicated his life could become if he didn't rein in his feelings, but he'd heard a plea in Jenny's terse statements about her father and former boyfriend. Was he the person to help her work through past disappointments? If he did find a way to counsel her, would he be doing it for his own benefit as much as for hers? Why did everything about Jenny Kincaid seem so complicated?

Chapter Seven

Jenny came into the church with a big box of donuts, her treat for the kids who'd come in early Saturday morning to clean the storage closet and paint it. They'd embraced the idea with more enthusiasm than she would have believed possible.

Cindy had found enough helpers to get the job done in one day. Dave Phelps had to work in his father's hardware store that day, but he persuaded his parents to donate enough paint to cover the shelves and walls of the closet. Emily and two other girls had gone to the store to pick the colors, and their choices couldn't have been better. The walls would be creamy white and the shelves a rich caramel brown.

Because only two or three people could work in the confined space at time, Mac had helped them remove the shelves and lay them on plastic drop cloths in the corridor for painting. He was bent over, stirring paint with a stick, but straightened when Jenny came up to him.

"That was quick," he said with a broad smile.

"I called ahead. The Donut Depot tends to sell out of favorite flavors. You can have first pick."

"I like them all. Let the kids take what they want first. I'm still amazed at how many turned out to help. You did a great job getting them here."

"It was more Cindy's doing than mine. She must have spent hours on the phone. Everyone she called volunteered to help in some way."

"Don't do that." He lowered his voice, and his vivid blue eyes locked on hers, adding to her confusion.

"Do what?"

"Give credit to everyone but yourself."

"I'm just being honest."

"No, you're being unnecessarily modest," he said in a voice only she could hear. "These kids really look up to you. They wouldn't be here otherwise. If this project flies, it's because of you."

"You're the one who persuaded the church council to okay it. Do you know how unusual it is for them to approve anything the first time they hear about it?"

"They're good people," Mac said, "but so are you."

One minute he was reprimanding her, and the next he looked at her in a way that washed away her objections like spring rain on a dusty roadway. She turned away, hoping that none of the young people noticed their exchange.

Mac hadn't meant to make her uncomfortable. He usually read people well. Insight into the feelings of others was one of his strengths as a minister, but Jenny confounded him. One minute she could be laughing and joking with the kids, then for no apparent reason a shadow of sadness would mask her features.

He knew now that she'd been badly hurt by men in her past, but was she naturally somber? He didn't think so, but he did know that her smile was special. When she smiled at him, he felt as if the sun had come out on a gloomy day.

"Hey, everyone," she called out, "I'll put these donuts in the library. There's soda there in a cooler. Help yourself whenever you like."

On impulse Mac followed her, watching as she put the box on a round table that served for meetings. The congregation called the room a library, but it was more a catchall for everything that didn't fit anywhere else. She had to move aside a box of Sunday school papers, a red umbrella and a box of crackers.

"I meant to thank you for all your work, not distress you," he said contritely.

"You didn't."

She wasn't a very good liar. That was another thing to admire about her.

"You remind me of an aid worker I knew. She worked her fingers to the bone to establish a center where women could feel safe in a very bad situation."

"Was she special to you?" Jenny didn't look at him when she asked.

"Maybe she could have been, but our careers took us in different directions too soon. I don't hear from her anymore."

"That's too bad."

He waited a moment, hoping she would trade confidences and answer some of the questions he had about her. Instead she busied herself finding a package of napkins in a cupboard and laying them out on the table.

Every movement she made was graceful. She'd dressed for work in faded jeans and a black Pittsburgh Pirates T-shirt, making him wonder whether she was a baseball fan. He really knew almost nothing about her, only that she was genuinely sweet, earnest and at least a little unhappy.

"How do you think your team will do this season?" he asked, realizing that they weren't going to have a personal discussion.

"What?" She looked up at him.

"The Pirates? Do they have a good team this year? I haven't been following baseball lately."

He could usually connect with men by mentioning sports, but it obviously wasn't going to work with Jenny.

"Oh, the shirt. I borrowed it from my sister because it already has some paint stains. I don't know much about the team."

And that, he thought to himself, is a strikeout.

By noon it was obvious that there was nothing more for him to do. Paint had to dry before the shelves could be installed. The hard-working kids gradually drifted away until only Jenny was left. She cleared away the empty donut box and was on her way out when he stopped her.

"It looks great," he said, gesturing toward the newly painted room. "It looks bigger since it's been repainted. Do you think we'll need more shelves? The church council offered to donate some start-up money if we need to buy some."

He realized he was chatting just to keep her there a bit longer.

"I think those will do for now, don't you? Better to use the money to buy some groceries. We have no idea what people will donate," she said.

"True," he agreed. "A supermarket near my dad's church had a sale on canned vegetables. People donated more than three hundred cans of peas and corn for the Thanksgiving baskets that year."

"Oh, no!" She laughed, and the sound was like music to his ears. "What did they do with all of them?"

"Shared them with the city's food pantry, although they had more than they needed, too."

"I've been thinking," she said. "The hard part will be finding people to distribute food during the day when kids are in school and most adults are at work."

"We'll have to set limited hours, maybe once or twice a week."

"Of course, you can hand it out whenever someone in need comes to you."

"Thank the Lord for that!" he said fervently. "Is there any chance you're free for lunch? I'd like to hear more about your plans for fundraising activities."

"Sorry, but I have to go right to work. Charlene did me a big favor by giving me the morning off. We're booked solid at the shop for the rest of the day."

"Well, maybe some other time," he said, surprised at how disappointed he felt. He hadn't intended to ask her out, but he still felt a bit rejected.

After she left, he wandered through the church and out to the recently tilled garden area. He needed to polish his sermon, but he felt too restless to settle down.

The morning had been a good one. He couldn't ask for more cooperative young people, and it looked like the whole church would get behind the emergency food pantry. It had been a pleasure to work with Jenny, even though her private life was as mysterious as her smile. Considering the short time he'd been there, he should be pleased with the way things were going. Still, he had vague doubts about where his place in the world was. Is this what God intended him to do?

* * *

The Lord must be pleased with their efforts if the beautiful Sunday morning in May was any indication, Jenny thought. It had been Mac's idea to have a little ribbon-cutting ceremony after the service to make the congregation more aware of the emergency food pantry. His sermon on the loaves and fishes had called attention to the needs of those less fortunate.

She admired him more all the time as a minister and knew their church was indeed blessed to have his leadership. But she wasn't at all sure how she felt about him as a man.

Her mother and sister had gone on ahead, but she'd stayed behind to lock up the pantry room and congratulate some of the young people on their good work before they left.

Mac had been busy with members of the congregation, and she thought it was best if she left before he was free. She admired him, but she didn't always like the way he made her feel. He reminded her of the things she was missing as a single woman.

She knew how it felt to be part of a couple, even though she'd probably been too young for a serious relationship when she started dating Jack. But the one thing she still missed about him was the security of always having someone to share her thoughts. They talked a lot, and she always had someone who would hear her side of things with an open mind. Sometimes she thought her mother, her sister and even her friends listened but didn't hear.

She slid her purse onto her shoulder, intending to go downstairs and out the rear exit. When she turned away from the pantry door, Mac was standing less than three feet away. He wasn't alone. Mrs. Hodges, one of the church leaders and chairperson of the committee that had hired him, was talking to him.

Jenny didn't exactly dislike the strong-willed older woman, but Mrs. Hodges's idea of Christian charity had been an embarrassment after Jenny's father had deserted the family. She'd arrived at their doorstep with a bundle of grungy, used clothing and a big bag of day-old bread she'd picked up on a trip to a nearby town. Her mother had tried not to show it, but the unwanted gifts had humiliated her. She worked hard to support her girls, and, to his credit, her father did make regular child support payments.

She decided to hurry past, but her attempt to avoid them was foiled. Mrs. Hodges turned aside from the minister and blocked her way.

"Jenny, I just invited Reverend Arnett for dinner Thursday. It would be so nice if you could join us too."

Jenny was dumbfounded. The Hodges thought of themselves as the first family of Pleasantville, and they'd certainly never invited anyone in the Kincaid family to anything. She didn't know how to refuse, but no way did she want to endure a stuffy meal in the big Victorian mansion on Charles Street.

"I thought we could have appetizers at six, if that works well for you, Reverend. It will be an informal meal, so no need to dress for dinner, Jenny."

Jenny was thoroughly miffed. The woman just assumed that she'd come.

She opened her mouth to refuse the invitation, but Mrs. Hodges didn't give her a chance, instead continuing her conversation with Mac as though Jenny didn't exist.

"Mrs. Hodges," she interrupted when it appeared that

the woman had forgotten her existence. "I'm sorry but I won't be able to come to your dinner. Thank you anyway."

Jenny thought it was a polite response to a very high-handed invitation. Apparently it surprised Mrs. Hodges. No doubt she didn't get many refusals.

"What a shame," she said. "I do hate a dinner party with uneven numbers. My mother always insisted that the number of ladies and gentlemen be equal. Well, perhaps Miss Dunning can fill in. I haven't had her over in some time. But I thought Reverend Arnett would enjoy dining with someone closer to his own age instead of just us old folks."

Jenny sighed but didn't change her mind. Now she understood the reason for the invitation. Mrs. Hodges had made no secret about preferring a married minister. She was an unlikely matchmaker for someone not in her social circle, but there it was. There weren't many single women close to Mac's age in the congregation. Mrs. Hodges had targeted her as a potential wife. Jenny was angry for his sake as much as her own. What gave the woman the right to interfere in their personal lives?

"I do have to be going," Mrs. Hodges said to Mac, ignoring Jenny and hurrying on her way.

"I'm sure she meant well," Mac said when they were alone in the corridor.

"For a world traveler, you're pretty naive," Jenny said, venting her indignation on him. "She wants a married minister. Apparently I'm one of her candidates."

"It was only a dinner invitation."

His reasonable tone of voice only made her more angry.

"She was trying to meddle. Don't you think I recognize matchmaking when I see it? I get enough from my mother and my sister and Charlene at the beauty shop and even my friends. I hold the Pleasantville record for the most blind-date offers in one lifetime. No one ever stops to think that I'm single because I want to be."

"Maybe you're the one who isn't thinking. The people in your life want you to be happy. Do you get this angry at everyone who tries to do you a favor?"

His question was a reasonable one, but it only irritated her more.

"A favor! Is that what you call matchmaking? Do you like people trying to manipulate you into a relationship?"

"No, but I take it in the spirit it's offered. I'm not ready to settle down into a permanent relationship—I don't even know where I'll be when my year here is up. But I don't see any point in getting mad about it. You don't have to go to dinner at the Hodges."

"I'm not mad, and I'm not going." She didn't like the way she sounded, but who was he to be judging her? "But don't underestimate Mrs. Hodges. She'll find someone to pair you up with at her dinner party, and it won't be the Sunday school superintendent. Miss Dunning must be double your age."

"I plan to call on every member of the congregation as time allows. This will count as my visit to the Hodges. I don't know why you're so agitated about it."

He sounded peevish for the first time since she'd known him. Apparently she'd made a mistake in thinking he was so perfect.

"I don't know why you feel you have to explain to me," she said, attempting to get around him and leave.

"Maybe I made a mistake thinking we could be friends."

"Can a man and a woman be friends? It certainly never worked out that way for me."

"How can you judge all the men in the world based on your limited experience?"

"Don't try your counseling techniques on me, Reverend Arnett. You don't begin to know me."

"I think that's the way you want it." He sounded hurt, but she was too upset to care. "You're not happy with the way your life is going, so you're trying to blame it on the men who've hurt you. Maybe you should step back and take a long look at yourself."

"Do you call this corridor counseling?" She looked around him, but they seemed to be the only ones left in the church.

"Catchy name," he said. "If you ever want to talk, you're more than welcome to call the church office for an appointment."

She hated that he'd backed away from personal confrontation and became the minister/professional counselor.

"Why do troubled people always want to solve other people's problems? Why do you think you have to travel halfway around the world to be useful to anyone?"

She looked at his clenched jaw and narrowed eyes and realized she'd gone too far. Did she really want to be at odds with this kind and caring man? Was there anything she could do to take back her angry words? He walked away before she could think of a way to make things right between them, but she very much didn't want him to think she was a terrible person. How could she repair the rupture with the one man who'd offered her real friendship?

Chapter Eight

At the youth meeting Wednesday evening, the kids were still excited about their work on the food pantry and full of ideas to keep it stocked. Mac wasn't there yet, but Jenny was able to sit back and let Cindy, the president, handle things.

"Now, how many think we should have a car wash after school is over for the year?" Cindy asked, counting hands as almost everyone voted yes.

"Good. Now who wants to take care of getting school board permission to have it in the high school parking lot?"

"If we have it there, will they let us use the water for free?" Dave Phelps asked.

"Good point, Dave. Will you be in charge of finding a place that will donate the water?"

"Yeah, I guess."

"I'll help," Emily volunteered, something Jenny knew Emily wouldn't have done before the horse farm brought her out of her shell.

Jenny's mind wandered as the meeting went on, wondering whether she was the one who needed to come out of a shell. Her life had settled into a comfortable rut: work, helping with Toby, church activities and an occasional evening out with Kayla and sometimes Kate, if her married friend could join them. It was a good life, but more and more lately, she'd felt something was missing.

There was a stir in the room, and she saw Mac walk up to Cindy, his face flushed as though he'd been running.

"Sorry to be late," he said without explanation.

He was wearing dark trousers and a white dress shirt with the cuffs buttoned, suggesting that he'd been busy with church business. Her first thought was that a member of the congregation had taken ill or been in an accident. It might be very comforting to have Mac nearby in case of emergency.

Cindy brought him up-to-date on what they'd been discussing—a good thing because Jenny wasn't ready to talk to him herself. Mac nodded approval as Cindy spoke, then congratulated the group on their willingness to continue helping.

"I have an idea," Mac said. "How many would like to go to the Strawberry Festival in Buckhannon a week from Saturday?

There was an instant stir of approval. The annual event was always held in May, and there was a lot to do there besides eat strawberries. Jenny hadn't gone in years, but she remembered all kinds of exhibits and activities, even a pie-eating contest.

"If everyone wants to go," Mac said, "we'll need some parents to drive. Jenny and I will work on that. Last I looked, your treasury had enough in it to ensure that everyone gets their fill of strawberry shortcake."

It was such a good idea that Jenny wished she'd thought of it. She knew that a successful youth group needed fun times and opportunities to get to know each other better in addition to worthwhile projects.

The meeting lasted longer than usual because the group had so much to discuss. When it was over, she waited outside the building until the last young person who needed a ride was picked up, then she started walking home.

"Jenny!"

She turned to see Mac hurrying to catch up with her.

"I thought that went well," he said when he came up beside her.

"Yes, that was a great idea of yours, the Strawberry Festival." Was he going to pretend that their last meeting hadn't ended badly?

"I haven't gone since I was a kid, but I remember having a lot of fun. One year I was runner-up in the strawberry capping."

For a moment she didn't know what he meant, then she remembered the contest where people tried to remove the tops of a quart of berries in the quickest time.

"And there won't be any horses," he gently teased.

Against her will, she felt a renewed surge of gratitude for his help in getting her through that ordeal.

"I seem to remember other rides, an old-fashioned steam engine, some carnival rides, hot air balloons. Nothing that bites or tosses people off, though," she said, not wanting to be the first to mention their hard words on Sunday.

"If you want to ride a horse on the merry-go-round, it will be my privilege to hold the reins," he said.

"I don't think that will be necessary."

"We do have a few things to work out," he said.

"Oh?" She wondered whether he meant personally or the trip plans.

"Chaperones to help with the driving, permission slips, maybe a few rules and a time schedule," he said. "But you know the routine better than I do."

"Yes." Besides being fun, a trip meant a lot of responsibility for the sponsors.

"I haven't had dinner. Would you mind coming to the Owl Café with me? We can go over the details while I eat—my treat if you want something."

"It's pretty late," she said hesitantly, not at all sure that it was a good idea to be alone with Mac.

"So it is." He glanced at his watch. "We could meet for an early breakfast, if you prefer."

"No, let's do it now."

If he wanted to pretend that nothing had happened to put them at odds, she would go along with his game—for now.

Mac led the way back to his car parked beside the church. He'd come from the hospital after spending time at the bedside of an elderly member of the congregation. Her life had hung in the balance throughout the afternoon, but by early evening his prayers and those of her loved ones had been answered. The crisis passed, and she'd lapsed into a healing sleep.

Mac wanted to tell Jenny about his experience, but he felt bound by an unwritten code of silence when it came to ministering to the congregation. One of the hardest things about his job, he was learning, was that he didn't have a confidant. Sometimes it meant everything to have someone who would listen. His mother did that for his father, and when Mac worked overseas, the mission workers often shared their feelings. Here he was getting to know a lot of people, but he still felt very much alone sometimes.

Jenny remained silent despite his attempts to draw her into conversation. He'd been upset about their exchange Sunday, but he didn't want there to be hard feelings between them. Maybe they would both relax in the casual atmosphere of the little eating place.

He pulled up in front of the small family-owned café on the edge of town, a place where miners came when their shifts ended. The food was plain but good, and the high-backed wooden booths gave an illusion of privacy. He would be proud to be seen anywhere with Jenny, but he'd deliberately chosen a restaurant where they probably wouldn't be recognized. He didn't want to make Jenny vulnerable to gossip.

"I haven't been here in ages," Jenny said as they settled down across from each other on black faux-leather seats. "When I was in high school, Jack liked to…" Her voice trailed off.

"Come here on dates?" He wanted to know more about her former boyfriend, but no way would he have brought him up first.

"After games, mostly. It was a popular hangout for jocks, but I don't know whether it still is."

"Did you date him very long?"

"All through high school. We even talked about getting married, but one day he said goodbye and I never heard from him again. I doubt that he's ever been back. His parents moved away a few years ago."

She flicked back a strand of hair that had fallen over her face and picked up the menu.

"You know, they used to have wonderful pie. Maybe I'll have a piece of Dutch apple if they're not sold out," she said, obviously wanting to change the subject.

"Jack's leaving must have been a disappointment," he

said, ignoring the menu, not willing to drop the subject of her past.

"I suppose, but I'm used to men leaving our family. My dad left us for another woman, and my sister's marriage fell apart while she was pregnant with Toby. I'm no believer in happily-ever-after."

She was talking in a flat monotone, surely an attempt to conceal the pain behind the words. He had an almost overwhelming urge to take her hands and offer some kind of comfort, but he realized it might stress her even more.

He'd always sensed that she was carrying around some serious hurt. He was both relieved and saddened by her unhappy experiences with men, but he didn't know her well enough to offer any meaningful consolation. His attempt to offer advice had only led to friction between them.

An elderly waitress in a yellow uniform and a little white apron came to take their order. Mac ordered the special of the day—vegetable soup and breaded cod in a bun. Hungry as he was, he was a lot more interested in talking to Jenny than eating.

"You haven't had a serious boyfriend since high school?" Maybe she thought he was intruding in her life, but everything about Jenny seemed important to him.

"No, but not because I still care anything about Jack. I imagine it would have been a disaster if we'd gotten married. We were too young, and we had practically nothing in common. He could never make up his mind what he wanted to do. One day he'd talk about joining the military, and the next he'd want to try his hand at stock car racing. I can't imagine following him from army base to army base or tagging along on the racing circuit."

Or from one mission posting to another, Mac thought, beginning to understand how firmly rooted she was.

Would she ever live anywhere but Pleasantville? He'd missed one opportunity to have a lasting relationship because Elizabeth was completely dedicated to her relief work, no matter where it might take her. Was there any chance that Jenny would follow him if he decided to take another overseas mission?

Mac could understand her devotion to her family and the town, but it didn't make him happy. The last thing he wanted to do was hurt her, but he didn't know whether he'd have a job when his interim year was up. Or whether he'd want to stay in Pleasantville. He should put Jenny out of his mind and spend as little time as possible with her, but he was afraid it was too late for that. He already cared for her more than he wanted to admit.

She raised her eyes to his across the table, perhaps a little embarrassed by her confidences, and he could feel his heart thumping in his chest. He wanted to be with her, but he didn't see a happy ending for the two of them together.

"Any ideas about getting chaperones for the Strawberry Festival?" he asked, belatedly remembering his excuse for asking her there.

"I'll get on the phone after work tomorrow. Parents are usually good about helping out it they can." Her tone was lighter. No doubt she was glad to move away from the personal conversation.

"Betty Jo will run off the permission slips. I'll ask her when she comes to work tomorrow morning."

"She's a gem," Jenny said. "I think she spends more time volunteering her time than she does working for pay."

"Yes, she's helped me a lot. This is my first church, and I still have a lot to learn."

The waitress brought his soup and crackers and

Jenny's pie. Jenny watched the woman leave but didn't pick up her fork.

"Now you know a lot more about me than I know about you," she said, looking directly into his eyes.

"I guess you could call me a preacher's kid, but I resisted the idea of being a minister myself until I'd nearly finished my undergraduate degree in social work. I realized that I had to be able to offer people something monumental to turn their lives around. The answer had been right in front of me my whole life: faith in Christ. From then on, I never looked back."

"Your father must be proud of you."

He laughed. "He won't admit it, but I think he programmed me for the ministry from the time I was two."

"I think my mother hoped I'd do more with my life than I have—maybe be a teacher or a nurse. Not that she ever tried to change my mind about being a hairstylist, but she expected me to get married and give her more grandchildren by now."

She sounded wistful, and he couldn't tell whether she regretted her single lifestyle.

"You're still young—I guess I don't know how old you are."

"Twenty-six. Some days it doesn't feel young."

"I'm thirty. I never thought much about getting old until I injured my ankle. Hobbling around like an old man made me more sympathetic to the elderly."

"You don't walk with a limp now."

"No, thanks to a good surgeon."

"I broke my arm once. I fell off the climbing bars on the school playground when I was seven."

Considering how much he'd thought about her, it seemed natural to be exchanging such basic information.

But then, he liked to think that he'd learned far more important things about Jenny. She was kind, and her faith meant a lot to her. She was willing to help others, even when it inconvenienced her. She was a tireless worker at the church, and family was very important to her. She adored her nephew and probably assumed more responsibility for his care than her sister had any right to expect. She was fun to be with and a natural leader with the young people of the church.

He sipped his soup, hardly tasting it as he concentrated on the woman across from him. He'd already let his interest in her go too far, but where did they go from here? Should he avoid social situations like this so neither of them would be tempted to get too involved? He couldn't see their lifestyles meshing in any meaningful way, but he didn't know whether he was strong enough to deny himself this unexpected chance for love.

He knew that he couldn't stand to hurt her the way the other men in her life had, but he couldn't promise to himself or to her that he wouldn't answer another call to some distant—and potentially dangerous— foreign mission.

He looked into her warm hazel eyes and felt like he was drowning. Should he be noble and walk away while he still could? Or should he try for the kind of happiness that only came from loving someone and being loved in return? That was the rub. Would she ever be open to a loving relationship?

"You're not eating your pie," he said, an absentminded comment because his thoughts were as painful as they were confusing.

"I guess I'm not as hungry as I thought."

Her voice was a husky whisper that he had a hard time

interpreting. Was she sorry for coming here with him? Did she see through his excuse for asking her? They could have settled the details of the Strawberry Festival in a two-minute conversation.

Maybe she was still angry because he hadn't seen the invitation from Mrs. Hodges as anything important. He shouldn't have probed her reasons for refusing, but the truth was that he really wanted her to go with him. Mrs. Hodges didn't intimidate him, but he truly liked being paired with Jenny.

He concentrated on the soup, not wanting to dribble it down the front of his white shirt. Whatever she thought of him, he didn't want her to think he was a slob. Somehow he managed to eat most of it, although he hardly tasted it.

He watched her put a tiny bite of pie on her fork and put it between her lips, fascinated by the dainty gesture.

"Is it good?"

"Yes, would you like to share it?"

"No, I still have a sandwich coming."

"Maybe I'll just take the rest home. It would be a shame to waste it."

He smiled and agreed. It didn't surprise him when they talked about church activities through the rest of his supper instead of more personal subjects. Did she regret confiding in him? He was more confused than ever about this lovely woman. He didn't have a clue whether they were meant to be more than casual acquaintances.

Jenny caught herself twisting her fingers together under the table. It had been a mistake to come here with Mac, and a bigger one to talk to him about Jack. Did he think she was interested in being more than friends? Was she?

At least she'd made it clear that she wasn't a woman who wanted to be a man's shadow, going wherever his whim took him. She wanted a life of her own. If that meant changing professions or towns, it would be her decision. She would never, ever, open herself to the kind of abandonment her mother and sister had suffered.

Easy to say, she thought to herself, but she was drawn to Mac like a moth to flame. He was the kindest, most warm-hearted person she'd ever met. When he focused all his attention on her, as he had this evening, she was mesmerized. His eyes were the bluest blue she'd ever seen, so bright that she shied away from his gaze. She had the irrational feeling that he could see into her soul, and she was very much afraid that her small-town girl persona could never live up to his expectations.

"Ready to go?" he asked.

"Yes."

Their time together had flown by. No way could they have been in the café for over forty minutes. Maybe, she thought regretfully, it would be better if they were never alone like this again. When he left Pleasantville, as she was almost sure he would, she didn't want him to take her heart with him.

The last thing he said when he dropped her off in front of her house was that he could hardly wait for the Strawberry Festival. Was he excited about it because they would be there together? She lay awake for a long time thinking about this and the time they'd spent at the Owl Café.

She didn't want to be in love with Mac, but was it too late? Was there any way to avoid the heartbreak that was sure to come if he left his temporary job at the Bible Church whether because his contract wasn't renewed or he felt the need to move on?

She had to discourage him by driving a wedge between them, one that he couldn't overcome. But was she strong enough? Could she ignore the way he made her feel?

Chapter Nine

Mac was grateful to Jenny for the good job she'd done in organizing the trip to the Strawberry Festival. She hadn't needed any help from him to round up transportation and chaperones. Dottie Phelps, Dave's mother, took quite a few kids in her large SUV, and Emily's parents joined the group and drove, although they were usually as shy as their daughter had been before she excelled at the horse farm. His only regret was that Jenny had driven her own car to Buckhannon instead of riding with him, but the turnout was so good that they'd needed both cars.

After some initial milling around, Jenny gave a short talk about not wandering off alone and being prompt when it was time to go home. They were to meet in front of the courthouse, a hundred-year-old Greek revival building with a red brick facade and stately white pillars and dome—an easy landmark to find. In the meantime, everyone had the freedom to wander the small town of seven and a half thousand people and enjoy all that the festival had to offer.

The young people gravitated to the carnival area while

Dave's mother and Emily's parents went off together to enjoy the arts and crafts show. Ordinarily Mac would have been drawn to the field where antique engines, tractors and cars were on display, but he lagged behind, only interested in Jenny despite his misgivings about where his feelings could lead.

"I should probably wander around and be sure our kids are behaving," she said when the others had scattered.

"They're not going to get in any trouble here," he said, suspecting that she was using her chaperone duties as an excuse to avoid him.

"I suppose not. I'm not used to being the one in charge. I have this urge to rope them all together like day-care kids out for a walk. Silly, I guess."

"Not at all." He wanted her to stay with him, but he wasn't sure how to invite her.

"It's too bad Pleasantville doesn't have a special event like this. I saw several churches with big banners advertising strawberry pancakes and strawberry shortcake. We could raise a lot of money for the food pantry from a crowd like this," she said, looking everywhere but at him.

He nodded, feeling tongue-tied, an extremely rare occurrence for him.

"I haven't been here in quite a few years," Jenny said.

"Me neither. It's an interesting town. Did you know it was founded by two brothers who lived in the hollow cavity of a sycamore tree?"

"You're kidding!"

"No, they were English deserters from Fort Pitt. The British army had the unfortunate policy of killing soldiers who bolted. The pair lived alone in the wilderness, hunting game and fighting off timber wolves and an occasional bear or mountain lion."

"That doesn't sound like a very good beginning for a town," she said, sounding genuinely interested.

Mac loved history, especially tales of West Virginia, his home state. He warmed to his subject.

"Eventually they ran out of ammunition and were forced to go back to civilization for more. Fortunately they found out that the heat was off. They weren't wanted for desertion anymore. One brother settled in Kentucky, but the other returned to his refuge on the Buckhannon River with his wife and other settlers. They called the first permanent settlement Bush's Fort."

"I've always wondered where the name Buckhannon came from."

She wandered down the street beside him, and it felt like the most natural thing in the world to Mac.

"If I remember right, it's the anglicized name for an Indian chief who hunted in the area."

He couldn't believe how good it felt to be in the foothills of the Allegheny Mountains on this beautiful late spring day. He felt more at peace than he had in a long time as bits and pieces of the state's colorful history came back to him.

"I don't think this town is as pretty as Pleasantville, but it has a more colorful history," Jenny said, seemingly as absorbed in her surroundings as he was.

"When you start digging around, most places have an interesting history," he said, then laughed at himself for sounding like a history teacher.

"Once when I came here on a school trip, our teacher said the town had something to do with Stonewall Jackson. He was a general in the Civil War, wasn't he?" she asked.

"Yes, one of the greatest Confederate generals. If I

remember my history right, his grandparents were among the original settlers, and his sister later lived here. She was a Yankee supporter, though, which must have upset him."

"Even families were divided by that war, weren't they? Imagine how awful it must have been here with the men going off to fight on opposite sides."

"This town has seen a lot of tragedy," he agreed.

"Yes, including that awful mine disaster a few years ago. That's not something people forget."

"Nor should they, not while families are still suffering from the loss of loved ones. I hope the local churches have effective grief counseling programs."

Mac had lived and worked in faraway places, but he couldn't remember a feeling of belonging like the one that washed over him now. Maybe he did have a calling here in the state where he'd grown up. He pushed aside the thought but knew that he would have to pray long and hard to make the right decision about staying—if he was given the opportunity.

Without intending to, he brushed against Jenny's arm, smooth and firm below the little cap sleeve of her bright yellow shirt. He had a sudden vision of walking through life with her as a loving companion. Again he felt a need for someone who loved the Lord as he did and could share his zeal for serving Him. Could that person be Jenny? He was tormented by indecision and, at the same time, drawn to her as he never had been to any woman.

"Is there anything special you want to see?" he asked, trying to bring his thoughts back to the here and now.

"What I like most is seeing how people enjoy themselves," she said. "How do you feel about the pie-eating contest?"

He gave an exaggerated groan, and they both giggled

for no special reason. It was a small crack in the wall between them.

"As long as I don't have to participate," he said.

"We could check out the strawberry blonde contest instead," she said, consulting the program they'd been given at the parking area.

"No thanks. I prefer honey blondes."

He was deliberately flirting and just a little disappointed when she didn't have a comeback. Sometimes he worried that she only saw him as the minister of her church, not a man who was beginning to have serious feelings about her.

Jenny felt a shock of pleasure when Mac's warm skin brushed against hers. His throaty voice had lulled her into a sense of well-being, and the casual touch reminded her of how much she enjoyed his company. Perhaps she should have joined the other adults to avoid being alone with Mac. The truth was, she liked being with Mac. It was as simple as that, or so she tried to tell herself. Certainly she wasn't trying to monopolize his time. Probably everyone on the trip wanted to get better acquainted with the new minister. They would catch up with the others, and he would have plenty of opportunities to mingle. For the moment, though, she was going to let herself enjoy the unusual pleasure of being with an attractive man.

He took her arm to steer her toward the muted sound of carnival music, and she was sorry when he let go a moment later.

The carnival was set up in a field on the outskirts of town, not a long walk because the town itself was small. It was typical of the traveling outfits that went from one small town event to another following seasonal events.

There were the usual games that challenged young men to show off and enough rides to keep all but the most avid thrill seekers happy.

Mac stopped at the ticket booth and bought passes for both of them, although Jenny protested.

"I can buy my own."

"You can, but you're not." His broad smile dispelled any hint of a macho attitude. "You're doing me a favor. Think how silly I'd look riding alone."

"Too bad they don't have a roller coaster. I haven't been on one in ages," she said.

"You surprise me."

"Why?"

"A woman who quakes at a pony ride but loves a coaster?"

"That monster I rode was as big as two ponies. With teeth and no seat belt!"

"I apologize. I shouldn't tease you about a genuine fear."

She didn't mind the teasing, but the warm, cozy atmosphere between them was disturbing. The more time she spent with him, the harder it would be when they parted for good.

One of their girls, Cindy, bounded up to them sounding breathless and excited.

"Have you seen Dave? I was supposed to meet him by the Tilt-A-Whirl."

"We just got here," Mac said.

"I haven't seen him," Jenny added.

Cindy's face was flushed, although the morning sun wasn't uncomfortably hot.

"Well, I suppose he's somewhere," she said with resignation.

Jenny felt a flash of sympathy for the girl. She was lively, cute and smart but not very successful with boys. Maybe at her age that wasn't all bad if she didn't pin her self-worth on her lack of boyfriends.

What about you? Jenny thought to herself. Did her growing restlessness have anything to do with her single status? Did she want that to change? Was it worth the risk of being hurt as her mother and sister had been? She didn't have answers. All she could do was enjoy the moment.

"What first?" Mac asked after Cindy dashed away from them.

"There's a ride I've never tried," she said pointing at a big wheel that spun around and around horizontal with the ground. "The UFO."

"The line isn't too long," he said, leading the way to the queue of mostly young people awaiting a turn.

He looked like one of the locals in jeans and a black polo shirt, and she couldn't help noticing that his hair needed a trim. Her fingers itched to do the job, but no doubt he'd go to the barbershop for his next cut.

The young man in charge of the ride was dressed entirely in green with greasy yellowish makeup that was already beaded with perspiration. He didn't quite cut it as a pseudo-Martian, but she gave him points for trying.

Mac offered his hand as they climbed up for their turn, then both of them fastened their seat belts. The ride was fast. The ground streaked past as some riders screamed in panic or pleasure. Jenny thought it was relatively tame, but her heart raced when Mac reached over and gently squeezed her hand. He released it as the ride slowed to a stop.

They took a turn on everything, even the carousel. She

picked out a bright yellow horse with a relatively sedate expression, and Mac mounted a fierce-looking black one. She was already a little dizzy from all the rides—or more likely from sharing them with Mac—so she wasn't disappointed when this ride was a short one.

"You were a marvelous equestrian," Mac said.

"I felt a little guilty making little kids wait while I rode."

He laughed softly and put his hand on the small of her back to guide her away from the carnival midway.

"Shall we go act our ages now?" he asked with a broad grin.

"My sister's birthday is coming up. Maybe I can find a gift for her at the craft show."

"The craft show it is," he said genially. "How is your sister doing? I haven't gotten to know her yet."

"She acts happy enough, but I think she's still hurting. Duane was the only boyfriend she ever had. They dated all through high school. It was a big shock when he dumped her, even though he was a bad husband."

Mac looked thoughtful. "My father's church had a support group for people who'd suffered a serious loss or setback. I'm thinking of starting something like that for our congregation and any members of the community who might want to participate. Do you think there would be any interest in it?"

She was flattered that he wanted her opinion, but she didn't have an answer.

"It might be worth trying," she said, feeling unhelpful.

When they reached the craft show, it was crowded but worth working their way past the many booths. Jenny bought a quilted purse for her sister that could double as a diaper bag. The sunflower pattern was cheerful and colorful, just the kind of thing Sandy liked.

"Hungry?" Mac asked as they left the craft area.

"I guess we can't leave without trying something with strawberries."

Was this turning into a date, because everyone else in their group seemed to have vanished? She still had strong misgivings about spending so much time with Mac, but her reservations were at odds with her emotions. She wanted to be with him.

There, I've admitted it, she thought, which was all the more reason to avoid him in the future. Nothing he could say or do would change the fact that he might leave as soon as his year was up.

"Let's see what these church people have cooked up," he said as they wandered up to a clapboard church with a tall steeple. The front lawn was bustling with activity as volunteers served people at long tables.

When Jenny tasted her first bite of pancake she was glad she'd passed up the funnel cakes and caramel apples that had tempted her at the carnival. It was easily the lightest, most luscious pancake she'd ever tasted, and the strawberries and whipped cream only added to its perfection.

Maybe anything would taste wonderful in Mac's company. She'd never expected to spend the whole day with him, especially not just the two of them alone. No one seemed to need them for anything.

"Those were so good, I wish I had room for more," Mac said when they'd finished.

There was music in the air, the vigorous beat of a marching band. Either they were warming up or the band contest had started. Jenny didn't want to miss a single event of this wonderful festival, but eventually they would have to meet their group in front of the courthouse.

"What next?" Mac asked.

"Your choice. I enjoy it all."

They wandered out to the exhibition of antique engines and tractors, and Mac was so fascinated that she came to share his interest. Time flew by, until they reluctantly decided that they had to start back toward the courthouse.

Earlier she'd had to hustle to keep pace with him. Now he was moving slower, obviously favoring his bad ankle. When she asked if it was bothering him, he made light of it.

They met their group and sorted out the riders. Jenny thought about Mac all the way home, feeling lonely without him even though her car was filled with chattering girls.

It wasn't good that she missed being with him. No matter how much she enjoyed his company, she couldn't think of him as a friend. But did she dare think of him in any other way?

Chapter Ten

June was the month for weddings, so Mac wasn't surprised that three were scheduled in the next few weeks. He felt especially good about the one this Saturday. Nicole Harris, the bride-to-be, had been the first person to seek his counseling when he began his ministry at First Bible Church. Her first husband had been killed in the military in Iraq, and it was a big step for her to remarry, although she cared very deeply for her fiancé. Now she seemed ready to put her grief aside and get on with her life.

How many members of the congregation were carrying heavy burdens and not seeking help for them? Mac had talked to the church council and gotten the go-ahead to begin a series of group support sessions, not only for the grief stricken, but also for anyone who was troubled. He was working hard with Betty Jo's help to prepare for the first one.

Meanwhile, he had a very different kind of trouble this fine Thursday. He'd been invited to Nicole and Brad's rehearsal dinner and urged to bring someone with him—a date. Even his favorite bride-to-be had joined the quest to find a wife for the preacher. He sensed—and Betty Jo pretty much confirmed—the general opinion that he'd be an even better minister if he had a helpmate.

There was only one woman he wanted to invite to the dinner. He hadn't been alone with Jenny since the Strawberry Festival a few weeks ago, but she was never out of his thoughts for long. This was the perfect opportunity to be with her, but he hesitated. He didn't want to put her in the awkward position of being the focus of rumors. If they started going out in public as a couple, the congregation would hear imaginary wedding bells.

He liked his job more with each passing week, but he didn't have any illusions. The old guard in the church still wanted a settled clergyman, a married one.

He lost the debate with himself—or maybe he won. Either way, he decided to ask Jenny to go with him. She was a bridesmaid and was included in the party anyway, but it would make the bride-to-be happy if they came together. Even numbers seemed to be a really big deal in this town. But more importantly, being with her would turn an obligation into a pleasure.

Purple-haired Nadine had volunteered to do Jenny's hair after the shop closed Friday, and Jenny was pleasantly surprised by the results. Her coworker had concocted an elaborate upswept style using some pretty butterfly clips Jenny had bought ages ago and never used.

Jenny decided she looked downright sophisticated with her sleek hairdo and practically new sapphire dress. She'd borrowed some silver heels and a matching clutch purse from her sister, but her outward appearance didn't mean that she felt right about going to Nicole and Brad's rehearsal dinner as Mac's date. Her first instinct had been to refuse, but Mac made it sound like an important favor to him. She could understand that he was tired of being the odd man out, always alone in a group. As a single woman, she'd often had that feeling herself.

She'd been a bridesmaid for Nicole's first wedding too, and sometimes she felt like a professional member-of-the-wedding-party. How many times had she stood up for old classmates and current friends, not to mention a few cousins? Her elderly great aunt Louise had once asked her why she was always a bridesmaid and never a bride.

Louise wasn't known for tact, even before she became a bit senile, but the question stuck with Jenny. She told herself that she'd chosen not to get involved with a man, and, truth be told, the choices in Pleasantville were pretty slim. She didn't want anything to do with Billy Brady, a cousin of Duane's who probably wouldn't treat her any better than Duane had treated her sister. Robert at the bank would have been happy to go to the rehearsal dinner with her, but making conversation with him was like straightening frizz from a bad perm.

The dinner was being held in a private room at Calhoun's, her favorite restaurant in town. It was close enough to walk, but Mac picked her up in his car. She was grateful for that small courtesy. Her sister's spike heels weren't made for teetering on cement sidewalks.

As soon as she entered the room festooned with crepe paper streamers, it became obvious that she and Mac were the only singles there. Nicole's mother welcomed them warmly and directed them to the appetizers set up on a separate table. Both of the bride's parents were radiantly happy, delighted that their only child was getting on with her life after the tragic loss of her young husband.

Jenny knew everyone there, so it was easy to make

conversation, but the men and women milled around until they were separated by gender. That was when baby stories began to dominate the women's conversation. Jenny had Toby tales to tell, but talking about a nephew wasn't quite the same as bragging about a child of her own. She was more than ready for the sit-down dinner to start when Mac came to claim her as his partner for the meal.

He'd gotten a haircut—about time actually—and he looked especially handsome in a fawn-colored linen jacket with a starched white shirt open at the collar.

"You look lovely tonight." He said it so quietly that only she could hear.

She wasn't used to compliments that meant something. His certainly did.

"Nicole and I are happy to see all of you here tonight," the groom-to-be said in a hearty voice that commanded everyone's attention.

Jenny liked Brad McCall, even though he had been one of the most boisterous boys in her graduating class. He was short on couth but long on goodwill. She thought he'd be a good husband for Nicole, and he certainly was nice looking with a thatch of yellow-blond hair, lively blue eyes and a weightlifter's broad shoulders.

Nicole's mother was calling for stragglers to find their places at the long, linen-covered table. When everyone was settled, Mac was called upon to say a blessing. Jenny didn't know whether he'd prepared it ahead of time, but she soon thought it was the most moving she'd ever heard, maybe because of the deep sincerity in his voice.

"Dear Lord," he'd said as everyone stood, bowed their heads and joined hands. "We're gathered at this table to celebrate the very special union of Nicole and Brad. Let everyone here, their friends and loved ones, pledge to support and sustain them in the years to come, trusting in You to bless their time together. Thank You for the bounty of this meal, for the fellowship of like-minded Christians and especially for Your eternal grace."

Jenny murmured "amen" with the others. She was deeply touched by Mac's appropriate prayer and immensely grateful that Nicole was able to put sorrow behind her and move on with her life. She'd always regretted not having a child, and Jenny silently prayed that her friend's life would be blessed with as many babies as she wanted.

She was so preoccupied that she remained standing while almost everyone else sat. It took her a moment to realize that Mac was holding her chair.

"That was a nice prayer," she said when she was seated beside him.

"Nice" seemed like an inadequate word, but Mac rewarded her with a small but grateful smile.

He seemed so much at ease, both in the pulpit and in social situations, that it had never occurred to her that he had any need of praise. This small hint of vulnerability made her like him even more.

A young server put a bowl on the plate in front of her, and she turned her attention to a tempting spinach salad with a zesty dressing hinting of lemon and savory mustard. Mac was talking to one of Nicole's aunts on his left, so she had a moment to study his hand as he reached for a fork. He had long, strong fingers and immaculately clean nails, not professionally manicured but nicely shaped. She'd always thought that people's hands told a lot about their character.

A leaf of spinach fell off her fork before she could carry it to her mouth. Wouldn't it be awful if she dribbled salad dressing down the front of her dress?

Why did being near Mac make her want to be more perfect than she was? She hadn't looked forward to this intimate gathering of the wedding couple's family and friends, but she'd never had any insecurity about her table manners. Now she was almost paralyzed by the thought that she might send bits of spinach and bacon coursing down the front of her best dress.

"Good salad," Mac said, taking his first bite and turning his attention to her.

"Yes."

"Have you and Nicole been friends for very long?"

"Since grade school."

"I like a morning wedding with a luncheon for the reception. I'm not much on dancing through the night, especially not since I injured my ankle."

"Oh," she said, wondering whether she was setting some kind of record as the dullest dinner companion ever.

She'd thought about Mac a lot since the Strawberry Festival, but now that she was face-to-face with him, she wasn't sure where their relationship stood.

It took forever for a server to clear away the mostly uneaten salad in front of her to make room for the main course. Mac made conversation with one of the groomsmen sitting across from him, and she could hardly blame him. Her conversation had all the sparkle of a muddy window.

The main course was chicken cacciatore, one of the restaurant's specialties. It was served with batter-dipped fried green beans and crusty rolls.

"This looks wonderful," Mac said to no one in particular.

Jenny looked at her plate. It was the first time she'd ever had a panic attack over food. She had visions of bright red sauce landing in her lap. She took a deep breath and tried to think of a reason for leaving the dinner without taking a bite.

"The food looks good, but I like the company even better," Mac said in a low voice that only she could hear.

She felt relief wash over her. It wasn't the food that spooked her. She was anxious because she wanted to be a perfect dinner companion for Mac. She wanted to be clever and amusing. She wanted to fascinate him with witty conversation.

What on earth was she thinking?

"Have you ever officiated at a wedding before?" she asked.

"Several times, but never in this country. In Haiti I married a couple and it was an affair for the whole village. I took some pictures thinking I could use them some time to stimulate interest in our mission program. I'd be happy to show them to you."

"I'd like that. I keep telling myself that someday I'll see more of the world, but…" She shrugged, not wanting to go into the reasons that kept her in Pleasantville. She had a small savings account, but at the rate it was growing, she'd qualify for senior rates by the time she went anywhere.

"I haven't told you about Mrs. Hodges's dinner." He looked around, lowering his voice to whisper.

"Were the numbers even?"

"Not exactly. I was outnumbered three to one. One niece, one secretary from her husband's office and a neighbor who lives with an invalid mother."

"She wanted to give you choices." Jenny giggled at the thought of Mac besieged by women herded together by Mrs. Hodges.

"What is it about women that turns them into rabid matchmakers?" he asked.

"They think men are happier if they're married," she suggested.

"More likely it's a power ploy," he said with a sardonic grin. "I found you a spouse, so you owe me."

"That's harsh!"

"Maybe," he conceded, smiling to show that he wasn't serious. "Anyway, I'm sorry you didn't go with me."

"Listen up, everyone," Brad said, standing to thank everyone who was involved in the wedding.

He gave special thanks to Mac. She was proud of him when he modestly accepted and made a small speech wishing the couple a long and happy union.

Thanks to the speeches, Jenny was saved from admitting that she was sorry about missing an opportunity to be with him. Something was happening to her, and she didn't know how to deal with her strange new feelings without risking a terrible disappointment if Mac left. Was she strong enough to live for the moment without anticipating future pain?

Jenny made Mac's evening when she smiled at him with her eyes as well as her lips after he made a short speech wishing happiness to the bridal couple. For the rest of the meal, he divided his attention between her and the others who sat around him, conscious of what was expected of him but constantly aware of her. In fact, he was so focused on her that he dropped a dab of tomato sauce on the front of his shirt.

He didn't embarrass easily, but he flushed when Jenny looked in his direction, catching him in the unsuccessful act of trying to rub it away with his napkin.

"I was sure I was going to do that," she whispered.

They both laughed, and he felt one step closer to her than he had when the dinner began.

The guests were having fun. It seemed no one wanted to leave, and Mac didn't want to be the first, although he badly wanted to be alone with Jenny. How conspicuous would it be if the minister whisked away one of the bridesmaids? He didn't care for himself, but he didn't want Jenny to be the object of speculation.

"There is something I want to talk to you about," he said when no one was paying any attention to them.

"The youth group?"

"No, you're doing great with that. Maybe in the fall some parents will step forward and help you. It's about a support group I'm going to start."

He knew that Jenny couldn't play a part in his plans, but he badly wanted her to confirm that he was on the right path. Her opinion meant a great deal to him.

"What kind of support?"

"Reverend, nice you could join us tonight," the groom's father interrupted, clamping his hand on Mac's shoulder.

"It was my pleasure," Mac said, standing to talk to him. "Great dinner."

The man moved on to circulate around the room. Some guests were leaving, and Mac took that as a sign to go himself.

"Are you ready to leave?" he asked Jenny.

"Yes, I think so. I'll just thank Nicole's mother for the nice dinner."

Leaving wasn't as easy as he'd hoped. They both had to work their way to the exit, engaging in short conversations with other guests. He thought of himself as a patient man, but he was getting downright antsy to be alone with Jenny.

At last they were in his car, driving to her house and stopping on the street in front of it.

"Thank you for the ride," she said, as though that was all there was to their evening together.

He was mildly disappointed but at a loss to know exactly what he'd expected from her.

"Maybe we can get together sometime soon," he said.

"We'll both be at the wedding," she reminded him.

That wasn't what he had in mind, but Jenny slipped out of the car without waiting for him to come around and open her door.

Maybe he was making too much of escorting her to the dinner. After all, they were the only single guests as far as he knew. He'd been almost sure that she was enjoying herself as much as he was, but it was clear that she had no interest in prolonging the evening.

What did he expect from her? Why would she invite him into her home when she had no way of knowing where a relationship between them would lead?

To put it the old-fashioned way, were his intentions honorable? What did he expect from her, and what did he have to offer? A year from now he might be tramping through a jungle or ministering to stricken refugees on the edge of nowhere. He might not have a choice about staying, but he wasn't even sure he wanted to. In his present situation, did he have any right to cultivate his friendship with Jenny?

He'd walked away from Elizabeth because the only other choice was to give up his ministry and join her secular relief agency. He seldom thought of her now, but he realized she hadn't touched him the way Jenny had. Where was this leading? He couldn't give Jenny up without leaving a painful void in his life, but he couldn't promise they'd always be together. His heart felt as if a heavy river rock was weighing him down, holding him back when he desperately wanted to follow her and tell her how much he cared about her.

Instead, he slowly drove away, wondering whether it would be best to leave Pleasantville now and spare them both the pain of a long and fruitless friendship. Was that what Jenny wanted from him? Could he force himself to do it even though it would be painful beyond anything he'd ever experienced? He drove until his gas was low and his spirits lower, finally heading for home when the dark summer sky was split by bolts of lightning and rain came down in torrents.

What should he do about Jenny? He didn't have a clue.

Chapter Eleven

"Work your magic, girlfriend," Kayla said, practically bouncing in Jenny's chair.

"You really don't need a cut," Jenny said, running a comb through her friend's hair.

"Well, fluff it or puff it or give it some highlights. Mom will have a fit if I don't make an effort to look good."

"Your mom has something planned for you? Come over to the sink, and I'll see what I can do after your shampoo."

"You know my mother, always trying to match me up with some guy," Kayla said, following Jenny and settling down to have her hair washed.

"What is she up to this time?" Jenny tested the water temperature on her wrist, then moistened her friend's hair.

"The preacher is coming to dinner."

"You have a date with Reverend Arnett at our church?" Jenny squeezed an oversize glob of shampoo onto her hand and let it slide between her fingers in surprise. Mrs. Hodges was bad enough as a matchmaker, but now Kayla's mother was stalking him. She was angry for his sake and unhappy with herself for caring.

"No, it's not a date, but Mom insisted on inviting him for dinner. What do you think he'd like better, chicken and dumplings or Mom's famous meatloaf with tiny new potatoes? She thinks I should know."

"I've no idea." Jenny squeezed out more shampoo and rubbed it into Kayla's hair.

The more Jenny thought about it, the more annoyed she became. Kayla fell in and out of love with every change of the seasons, but a crush on Mac could only lead to disappointment. It wasn't fair of her mother to push them together. She didn't want Kayla to be hurt, but she was irrationally upset by the idea of Mac spending time with her.

"Well, I picked the meatloaf. Mom puts in green peppers and onions and makes a crusty top with Parmesan cheese. I thought of doing steaks on the grill, but I wanted it to seem like an ordinary family dinner. You know, cozy and friendly."

Jenny was so lost in thought that she hardly heard her friend as she automatically finished the shampoo and led the way back to her station. She didn't have any right to object to Mac having dinner at Kayla's house, but she was upset anyway. She didn't think she was jealous—after all, she had no claim whatsoever on Mac. She did feel empty inside, as though someone had given her a wonderful gift, then snatched it away. This made no sense at all, but neither did the way she felt about him. There was no future for them together, but it hurt to think that someday he would find someone else to love.

He'd wanted to talk to her about something, or so he said at the rehearsal dinner. But she'd seen him at the wedding and at church the next morning, and he hadn't said anything personal. She didn't know what she'd do if he deliberately put distance between them. Just thinking about it was hurtful. She thought they'd become friends, but friendship wasn't nearly enough. Sometimes she wished he'd never come to Pleasantville. Her thoughts were in turmoil, and she couldn't seem to get him out of her mind, no matter what she was doing.

Kayla chattered on, not deterred when Jenny answered in a dull monotone or not at all. She worked automatically, hardly aware of what she was doing.

"It looks great!" Kayla said as Jenny lightly sprayed the results. "For once Mom has lined up a guy with potential. Wish me luck."

"Good luck," she said with a lack of enthusiasm Kayla didn't notice.

When Kayla left, Jenny felt drained. She wasn't booked again until after lunch, and she didn't feel like waiting around in case someone walked in without an appointment. It was only eleven, but Charlene didn't object when she asked to take an early break.

The soda fountain in the drugstore didn't offer much in the way of lunch, only rather tasteless sandwiches made up ahead and warmed in a microwave, but Sandy was working this morning. She could rely on her sister to distract her from thoughts about Mac. Her sister rarely quizzed Jenny about her life, but she was full of conversation about everyone else's business, including her own.

Jenny was the only customer when she sat down on one of the soda fountain stools. Sandy was stocking shelves, but she came over as soon as she saw her sister.

"What's up?" she asked.

"Just taking an early lunch break."

"You don't want one of our sandwiches," Sandy said, wrinkling her nose. "I brought a tuna salad from home. I'll split it with you."

"Thanks, but I thought I'd treat myself to a milk shake instead."

"Doc just mixed up a fresh batch of pineapple syrup, if that's what you want," she said referring to the pharmacist and storeowner by his nickname.

"Sounds good."

She watched as her sister scooped out ice cream and added syrup and milk. Working the soda fountain wasn't Sandy's favorite job, but fortunately for her, another clerk usually took care of it.

"I've been meaning to tell you something," Sandy said as she put a glass of thick, creamy milk shake in front of her. "I've been stewing about Duane for too long. I've decided to join the support group Reverend Mac is starting."

"What?"

"You know, a group where people can work out what's bothering them. There was an insert in Sunday's bulletin and a poster on the bulletin board."

"I must have missed them." Jenny tasted the milk shake, but it soured on her tongue.

"I don't see how you could have," Sandy said, more puzzled than critical.

"I just did."

She wasn't going to explain to her sister that she'd been preoccupied thinking about Mac, not understanding why he was so attentive at the rehearsal dinner but hadn't followed through on what he wanted to talk about. More importantly, why did she care so much?

"It starts Thursday evening. I'm really curious to see how many people come. You don't want to come with me, do you?" Sandy asked.

"I don't have any unresolved issues," she said, unintentionally snapping at her sister.

"I wasn't suggesting that you do. I just need a little moral support."

"Take Mom," Jenny said, trying to sound more helpful.

"Maybe I will. She didn't seem opposed to the idea."

Apparently Jenny was the only one in her family who didn't know what Mac was doing. Was the support group his reason for wanting to talk to her? If so, why had he changed his mind?

She picked up the glass and gulped down three large swallows of milk shake so quickly that it hurt her head. She'd had all the conversation she wanted to have with her sister.

"If you're not interested in going, can I count on you to watch Toby?"

"Yes, I guess so."

"I need to know for sure."

"Yes, okay, for sure. I have to get back to work." She laid the money for the milk shake on the counter and slid off the stool.

"Is this all the time you get for lunch?" Sandy asked, sounding ready to storm the beauty parlor and demand a longer break for her sister.

"No, but I have a few errands to do."

Number one on her list would be a painkiller for the headache building behind her eyes, but no way did she want her sister to know she had one. Sandy had worked at the drugstore long enough to think she was qualified to prescribe over-the-counter drugs. Worse, she would want to analyze the reason for Jenny's aching head.

Jenny escaped from her sister's protective care but didn't want to go back to work before she had to. It was downright hot out, and without a hat, a long walk would leave her red-faced, not to mention what it would do to her aching head. The only refuge downtown was the public library. She headed there in search of a quiet sanctuary where, hopefully, her headache would ebb away.

The reading room in the old Carnegie library, donated by the wealthy industrialist over a hundred years ago, was one of her favorite places. The town had modernized the library, one of nearly three thousand built by Andrew Carnegie, but had kept the stained glass windows and high vaulted ceiling that made it special.

She picked a magazine at random and sat down beside an empty table. There weren't many people, only a few older men reading the daily newspapers and a young couple who were obviously more interested in each other than in anything the library had to offer. Jenny resisted the urge to put her head down on the table to rest and opened the magazine to give the impression that she was reading.

She didn't hear the footsteps muffled by carpeting, but she couldn't help but be aware of a chair pulled out beside her.

"Mind if I sit here?" a familiar voice asked.

She looked up into Mac's intense blue eyes.

"No, it is the public library." She didn't mean to sound snippy, but it came out that way.

"So it is." He didn't sound in the least offended. "I haven't had a chance to talk to you lately."

She thought he'd had plenty of chances but didn't say so.

"My sister said she's going to your support group."

"Yes, she talked to me about it. I'm happy to have her. We have seven people so far."

"My mother may come too."

"She would be very welcome. So would you."

"Me?" She was genuinely shocked. "I don't have any reason to go."

Unless, she thought gloomily, it was the way she felt about the new minister in town. Mac was the last person she would tell about those feelings. In fact, she wasn't even sure how she did feel about him.

"No, but family members are welcome to sit in or even participate. I'm sure your insights would be helpful."

"I'm not comfortable with the idea of discussing my family's personal problems."

"I can understand that, but everyone who comes to the group will be asked to pledge not to reveal anything that's discussed."

"You have more faith in the people here than I do. Gossiping is the town's favorite recreation."

"It's not all bad for people to be interested in each other."

He was sounding like a preacher. She liked him better as a dinner companion. Or maybe her throbbing head was making her cranky with the world.

"You don't look well," he said in a kind voice that made her anger evaporate.

"Just a little headache."

"Would you like me to drive you home? I have my car outside."

"No! I mean, I have to go back to work."

"I know a technique that relieves most headaches." He stood and stepped behind her, placing one finger on either side of her eyes and gently massaging.

"Feel that little indentation right here," he said, guiding her finger up to replace one of his. "Just rub softly. There, that's it. How does that feel?"

"I feel a little silly, if you want to know the truth," she said removing her finger.

She also felt the pain lessen as he continued to massage, but she didn't say so. His touch felt too good to risk having him stop.

The young couple left the room, but Jenny was pretty sure she'd heard a stifled giggle as they passed her table.

"That's fine," she said. "It helped a lot. I'll have to remember that trick. My mom gets headaches sometimes, but I hardly ever do. I drank a cold drink too fast. That's what started it."

He sat down again, showing no sign that he was going to leave anytime soon.

Mac didn't feel good about the last couple of days. He thought about Jenny constantly, but he'd changed his mind about running ideas past her. He didn't want to put her in the awkward position of knowing more about the support group than she would want to know. It was a good decision, especially because her sister had been one of the first and most enthusiastic people to sign up for it.

He owed her some kind of explanation, but he didn't know how to go about it. He'd realized that he couldn't discuss church business with her the way his father had with his mother. It implied intimacy and trust between them. It would mean admitting he had strong feelings for her.

Nor could he say that he felt ready to take their relationship a step further, when he wasn't even sure they had a relationship. She was on his mind constantly. He couldn't just walk away from her, not without knowing whether they belonged together. In his whole adult life, he'd never been so indecisive.

"The library has a pretty good collection for a small town," he said for something to say.

"People here do read a lot."

She was studying her thumbnail. He noticed how small

and vulnerable her hands seemed. She was a delicate woman despite her height, and he wanted to protect her from all the hurts the world could inflict.

Conversation came easily to Mac, but not when he was with Jenny. He felt tongue-tied and awkward. He wanted to say something that would keep her there beside him, but words failed him.

"I have to go back to work," she said, standing and pushing her chair away.

"I'll walk you there."

"No, really, you don't need to."

"I have some errands to do in that direction."

It was the first time he'd told her an outright fib, but he didn't want to be away from her just yet. He'd come to an important realization. He had to see more of Jenny before he could come to any kind of decision about his future. They scarcely knew each other. If he left things as they were, he might regret it for the rest of his life.

The first step was to ask her on a date, a real one, not a church activity that threw them together because they were both involved.

"Tonight…" he began, then remembered that he'd already accepted a dinner invitation.

"What?" she asked as she led the way to the exit.

"I forgot I have a dinner invitation tonight. I was hoping we could get together sometime."

He ran through the week's activities in his head. Wednesday was the youth group, Thursday he was starting the support group and Friday his parents were coming for the weekend. He absolutely could not ask Jenny to help entertain them. His mother was so eager to see him married that she would overwhelm Jenny with attention.

"Are you asking me for a date?" She stopped and looked at him.

"I was hoping to, but I have my parents coming this weekend. They want to hear me preach."

"Any parents would be proud to have a minister as a son."

"Sunday evening, after they've gone?" he tentatively suggested.

"I'm not sure. I'll have to check with Sandy and Mom. I may have promised to babysit Toby."

Was she brushing him off? He felt vaguely hurt, but then, he deserved it. He hadn't talked to her much last weekend, although the last thing he ever wanted was to ignore her. He was just confused and wary of hurting her if they became too close.

The walk to the beauty salon wasn't nearly long enough. He gave up trying to find an evening when they could do something together, at least for the present.

"Thanks for showing me your headache cure," she said before she went inside. "I think it actually helped."

Now he had to figure out how to help the ache in his own heart. Should he continue trying to see more of her, or should he put distance between them to clarify how he felt? Above all, he didn't want to hurt her in any way, but how could he avoid that?

Chapter Twelve

The deluge started with a brief thunderstorm on Friday, but it was nothing compared to what followed on the weekend. By Sunday it seemed like an ocean of water was falling on West Virginia.

Mac watched from the church door as people hurried to their cars under a bobbing panorama of brightly colored umbrellas. The asphalt parking lot was a maze of puddles even though the First Bible Church sat on high ground.

He'd driven to the service himself, since the alternative was to arrive soaked to the skin. His mission work hadn't called for an umbrella because he rarely wore anything dressier than a pair of jeans. If he stayed in West Virginia, he might have to rethink owning one.

Jenny was among those racing across the parking lot, and her little collapsible umbrella wasn't doing much to keep her dry. The rest of her family waited until she pulled the car close to the church door, then made a dash to get in it. Little Toby had been quiet throughout the service, as far as Mac noticed, but now he was howling to escape his mother's arms. Like any energetic soon-to-be-toddler, he must think water puddles were for play.

"I can't remember when I've seen rain like this," Kayla Burns said as she stopped for a word before plunging into the weather.

"Yes, it is unusual," Mac agreed, shaking her hand as he did with all the members of his congregation.

"We really enjoyed having you come for dinner this week," the vivacious young woman said. "I hope we can do it again sometime."

"It was my pleasure," Mac said, deliberately noncommittal about a return engagement.

"Mom was thrilled that you liked her meatloaf. She got the recipe from her mother. In fact, it may have been in our family for generations."

Mac liked Kayla, but he knew this conversation wasn't about meatloaf. The last thing he wanted to do was give her false encouragement. He looked beyond her and saw that she was the last member of the congregation to leave.

"If you'll excuse me," he said, "I have my parents waiting in my office."

"Your father is such a dignified man, so handsome for his age," Kayla said.

"I'll tell him you said so," Mac said with a somewhat forced smile.

He certainly wasn't the first bachelor preacher to have this problem, but he didn't know how to discourage Kayla without hurting her feelings.

Today someone did it for him. Jenny's car circled the parking area and again pulled up close to the door, sending torrents of water splashing toward them. She just missed soaking Kayla.

"Silly me," Gloria Kincaid said as she dashed from the

car to the building. "I left my best Pyrex pan in the kitchen, and I need it to bake brownies for my book group."

Jenny's mother passed between Mac and Kayla, and he used the interruption to hurry down the corridor to his office.

Jenny hadn't wanted to come back for her mother's pan, but when Gloria got an idea in her head, it was useless to resist. She especially didn't like interrupting Kayla's conversation with Mac. She wasn't competing for his attention. She didn't want Kayla to see her as a rival. After all, they'd been friends for ages, and they would still be friends long after Mac left.

Toby was sobbing in his car seat, and Sandy was unsuccessfully trying to pacify him with bits of dry cereal.

Is this all there is to my life? Jenny thought in a rare moment of discontent. She adored Toby, and she loved her mother and sister. Still, she couldn't shake the nagging feeling that she was meant to do more with her time on Earth.

She saw Mac look toward her, but the rain beating against the car windows made it impossible to see his expression. Then he was gone, and Kayla was sprinting toward her car in the parking lot with only an offhand wave in Jenny's direction.

Mac's parents had sat in the front pew, and Jenny had joined her family in the rear area reserved for the parents of small children. Her only impression of the Arnetts had been positive, though. They were silver-haired and well dressed, but more importantly, they seemed overjoyed at hearing their son preach. He introduced them after the service, and they chatted with members of the congregation like old friends.

Now she knew where Mac got his charm and poise as

well as his dedication to others, but it didn't make her any happier. If he wanted to advance his career, he could easily move on to a larger church in a city like Charleston or Morgantown. Or, more likely, if he wanted to return to foreign mission work, he probably would be welcomed with open arms. Either way, his time in Pleasantville was probably limited.

Gloria came scampering back with her pan clutched against her, and Jenny headed for home.

Mac hadn't had an opportunity to introduce Jenny to his parents. Even though he knew his mother was marriage-minded, he'd wanted to see their reaction to her. He trusted their judgment about people, which was more than he could say about himself these days. Jenny was constantly in his thoughts, but he couldn't come to any kind of decision about what to do.

"I'm so glad you found a nice church," his mother said when they were preparing to leave for home after lunch at Calhouns. "The people seem so friendly. It's a good size congregation to begin your ministry."

Mac knew his ministry had begun when he accepted his first overseas assignment, but his mother's hopes for him had never been a secret. She wanted him to follow in his father's footsteps, perhaps someday becoming the minister in the church where her husband had served for many years. She supported his missionary work but saw it as a prelude to his real life's work.

"Good sermon," his father said. "I remember giving a similar one some years ago."

"Busted," Mac said, although he had no memory of his father's Good Samaritan sermon.

His mother wanted to leave because driving through

the rain on the hilly, twisting roads made her nervous. His father would stay and discuss things for hours if Mac gave him an opening. He admired his father, but he couldn't help noticing his tendency to pontificate since he retired from a full-time ministry. Thankfully he was a popular substitute preacher and keeping busy with hospital and nursing home visits. He had too much energy to settle into a life of inactivity.

"We'd better be going," his mother prompted.

Mac hugged both his parents, genuinely glad that they'd had a chance to visit his new church. He thanked the Lord that they had a strong, nurturing marriage. His father's ministry had made many demands on his mother, and she'd always risen to the occasion, whether it was baking a few hundred brownies for summer Bible school or visiting the congregation's shut-ins.

Would he ever find a helpmate like his mother? He could only imagine how fulfilling it would be to have a partner who would work side-by-side with him in spreading word of the Lord's grace.

The continuing rain kept him indoors all afternoon, but he was too restless to stay in his small house. He went back to his office, intending to tackle the endless pile of paperwork on his desk. Instead he went into the church, made gloomy by the gray skies outside. The downpour drummed onto the roof of the church, and he found himself praying in rhythm to its cadence.

He thanked God for his many blessings, not the least of which was a mother and father who'd loved and nurtured him as he grew up. He prayed they would get home safely, then beseeched the Lord to watch over his congregation and the many people he'd met during his overseas ministry.

Mac felt refreshed after his long prayer session, but he hadn't asked the Lord to resolve his greatest dilemma: what to do about Jenny. Somehow he knew that this answer would have to come from his own heart.

By the time he was ready to leave the church, it was nearly dinnertime. Cooking wasn't one of his gifts, and he didn't want to go home and thaw another frozen dinner. Still, his stomach was growling, and the Owl Café was closed on Sunday. He didn't feel like going to a nice restaurant by himself.

There was only one person with whom he wanted to share his meal.

"The worst she can do is say no," he said aloud, his words sounding hollow in the empty church.

The natural thing to do was call her, but he didn't want to be refused on the phone. Sometimes the mischievous boy who still resided deep within him surfaced, and this was one of those times. He would go to her house. If she didn't take pity on a rain-soaked, woebegone creature like him, she wasn't the Jenny he thought he knew.

Jenny was surprised that both her sister and mother had plans for the evening. She would be spending the evening with Toby. He was the delight of her life, already trying to walk before his first birthday, but she knew her sister took advantage of her affection for her nephew. More and more, Sandy just assumed that Jenny was available to take care of him. Partly it was her own fault for not having a more active social life, but Toby needed more attention from his mother.

After her mom and Sandy went their separate ways, she plopped him into his high chair, buckled him in and slipped a bib over his head. Feeding time was a messy time with Toby, and she spread an old plastic tablecloth around his chair to avoid having to mop the floor if he was in a playful mood.

Because Sandy hadn't said anything about what to feed him, Jenny found his favorite prepared toddler foods, spooned them into his dish and warmed the macaroni mix and carrots in the microwave. She tested the temperature on her wrist to be sure they weren't too hot, then tackled her least-favorite Toby job.

The little rascal was halfway between feeding himself and needing to be fed, and sometimes he ended up with more food on his face than in his tummy. She was wiping his mouth before going on to the applesauce course when the doorbell rang.

"Here, sweetie," she said, handing him an arrowroot cookie to keep him occupied while she ran to the door.

She opened it and didn't know what to say. Mac was dripping rainwater on the doormat with a sheepish grin on his face.

"You never know what a storm will wash up."

"Why are you here?" She wouldn't make hostess of the year with a question like that, but she was dumbfounded.

"I always wanted to do that Gene Kelly dance, 'Singing in the Rain,' so I parked down the street and gave it a try. Trouble was, I don't own an umbrella."

"The neighbors will think you're crazy!"

She couldn't help herself. She laughed with him until she was doubled over with mirth.

"Oh, I left Toby alone!" She sprinted toward the kitchen, leaving Mac to take off his shoes and drip on the indoor mat.

Toby hadn't missed her. He'd managed to reduce his arrowroot to a pulp that covered his face ear-to-ear. She grabbed a washcloth and began the cleanup without much hope of sponging it out of his fine dark hair. She didn't know who needed her attention more, the sticky baby or the soggy man.

Mac came into the kitchen, looking a little dryer on top, where he'd been wearing a rain jacket. His jeans, though, were soaked from the knees down, still dripping on the tiled floor.

"I actually came to ask you out for dinner," he said.

They looked at each other and began laughing again.

"I have to babysit Toby."

"He can come with us."

They both looked at Toby and laughed again until he began to whimper.

"It's okay, sweetie," she said, picking him up, messy bib and all. "Reverend Arnett is only kidding. He won't make you go out in all that rain. You're headed for a nice warm bath."

Mac's socks were making wet prints on the kitchen floor, and his jeans were uncomfortably clammy. His hair was plastered to his head, and he could feel the rain that had leaked down his back under his shirt. Jenny hadn't kicked him out immediately, so maybe she was a little bit glad to see him.

"I'll throw you down some bath towels to dry off," she said, carrying the baby toward the stairs.

He retrieved the towels and dried off as well as he could, pacing the kitchen to air-dry his jeans. After what seemed like ages, Jenny came back without the baby.

"With any luck, Toby is down for the night. Are you hungry?"

"Famished. How about I order a pizza?"

She hesitated, then agreed.

"It will be half an hour," he said after making the call for a delivery. "I'm not stopping you from anything you need to do, am I?" He wasn't sure whether he was a welcome guest, or she was only being polite by agreeing to share a pizza. At least they'd laughed together. That made him feel better about dropping in on her.

"It's okay. Did your parents enjoy their visit?" she asked.

"They seemed to. I'm sorry you didn't get to meet them."

"I avoided it."

Her honesty startled him.

"What? Why?"

She sat down across from him at the old-fashioned oak table. He didn't think she was going to explain, but after a few moments of silence, she shrugged her shoulders.

"They scared me a little."

He couldn't have been more surprised. It never occurred to him that anyone would react to his parents that way.

"They look so dignified," she went on, "but maybe a little judgmental. I was afraid they'd think I was a predatory female. You know, bachelor minister, single woman…"

"They wouldn't think that!"

He wasn't so sure about his mother, though. She wanted him to get married and give her lots of grandbabies. As an only child, he was her hope for the big family she hadn't been able to have. He'd always known her expectations. Maybe that was part of the reason why he'd chosen to begin his career in the mission field. But when he'd seen the great need in some of the world's poorest countries, he'd pretty much forgotten about his mother's plans for him.

"I'm sorry if I misjudged them."

"Well, you're not entirely wrong," he said, smiling to

reassure her. "My mother would love to see me married with lots of kids for her to spoil."

"But that's not what you want for yourself?"

"Someday," he said. "But if I go back into the mission field, I may be assigned to places that are too hazardous to bring a family. Anyone who married me could have a pretty uncomfortable life."

"That sounds like a warning."

"If circumstances were different—"

"You don't have to explain to me," she said. "I understand."

"I don't think you do." He was botching the whole conversation. He needed time to come to a decision about his future, but she was taking it as rejection. "I think you're a wonderful person, Jenny."

"But?"

"But what?"

"There's always a 'but' when a man tells a woman she's a wonderful person," she said, busying herself setting out plates and pouring iced tea so she didn't have to look at him.

He shook his head, not sure how to answer her.

"You are a wonderful woman. I'm afraid there will be a terrible void in my life if I miss out on the opportunity to get to know you better."

"Maybe I'm afraid too, afraid of you."

He couldn't have been more surprised it she'd sprouted a second head. He knew himself pretty well, but it had never occurred to him that he would frighten anyone, least of all the woman across from him.

"You have no reason…"

"No, of course not. It's not you. It's more what you stand for."

He was even more puzzled.

"What?"

"Change, I guess. I want my life to change, but I don't feel ready for it. I don't know what I want."

She sounded so unhappy that it was all he could do to keep from crossing the space between them and taking her in his arms. He sensed that it wasn't what she wanted, not here and now, but did they belong together? Would they ever bridge the differences between them? Was she the woman he wanted as his companion for life, or was he overly eager to find someone because he was lonely?

He thought about her words and realized that they shared one thing: they were both unsure about what direction their lives should take. What did the Lord have planned for him? Did Jenny figure in His plan?

"You don't have to make any decisions that will affect the rest of your life right now," he said in a soothing voice, talking as much to himself as to her. "I'll be here for the rest of my year. We have time to get to know each other better."

"It's easy for you to say. You're not torn between who you are and the things you want to do with your life. I've lived here forever. I'm afraid of staying and afraid of leaving. Sometimes I tell myself that my family needs me, and other times I think Sandy and Mom depend on me too much. It's not right for a minister to get involved with someone as confused as I am."

"You're selling yourself short," he protested, rising from the kitchen chair, intending to take her in his arms.

Her eyes were moist with tears, and he was sure of only one thing: he loved Jenny.

"No, don't," she said, backing away from him. "If you're nice to me now, I'm going to bawl like a baby, and I don't even know why."

The back door was flung open, and Gloria came into the kitchen, stomping to shake off rain.

"I swear, this must be a fifty-year rain. I can't remember ever seeing it keep up so long."

She looked up and saw Mac. To her credit, she didn't show any surprise.

"Hello, Reverend Mac. Nice to see you. I was listening to the radio on my way home. We're fortunate here, no major flooding yet, but some of the towns south of here are in a bad way."

"They're going to need a lot of help when this rain stops," he said, glad to address a problem he could do something about.

"I imagine our church will pitch in," Gloria said.

"Even the young people will be able to help in some way," Jenny said, perhaps wanting to give her mother the impression that they had been talking about the youth group.

Mac left a few minutes later, forgetting about the pizza that hadn't arrived. He took with him a better understanding of why Jenny had been leery of meeting his parents. She knew better than he did that a casual friendship between them was impossible. She'd been spooked by too many high-handed matchmakers to be introduced to his mom and dad as though she were someone special in his life.

When a mother had marriage on her mind, she went into matchmaking mode. He hoped Gloria, unlike Kayla's mother, wouldn't invite him for meatloaf. He and Jenny had a lot to work out, but pressure from other people would only make it harder. Would they ever be able to reach a point where love could blossom between them?

Chapter Thirteen

Mac hated to work on his sermon at the last minute, but early Sunday morning he was still struggling to flesh out his theme, the calling of the disciples. He wanted to make the point that the Lord still summoned the faithful to do His work, but Mac's mind was too full of all that he had seen and done in the past two weeks to do justice to the message.

The flood had indeed ravaged some towns, and none more so than Dillard, West Virginia, sixty miles south of Pleasantville. The river that ran through the town was usually shallow and placid, but rainwater rushed down from the surrounding hills, turning it into a raging torrent. The banks overflowed and flooded the business district, then spread to all the homes to the east and south. By the time the stormy weather passed, more than half of the town's residents were homeless. Almost no one escaped without some damage and debris to clean up.

Mac was proud of the way his congregation had responded. Mrs. Hodges used her considerable influence to gather truckloads of food, clothing and building supplies. The First Bible Church had sent a caravan to Dillard every day since the extent of the flood damage was known. Volunteers included several unemployed miners and retired people willing to donate their time. Mac hurried back and forth, working with the American Red Cross and other agencies as they struggled to sanitize and make habitable as many residences as they could.

George Darlington, the president of the congregation, had willingly agreed to let Mac postpone all his nonessential duties to work on relief efforts. George had personally made ministerial visits to the hospital and nursing home in his place, and his wife had gone to Dillard several times to help serve hot food to the homeless who were sheltering in the high school auditorium.

Jenny had gone several times, working at whatever jobs came her way. The last time he'd seen her in Dillard, she was wearing knee-high boots and rubber gloves, struggling with others to clear away rubble that blocked the front door to a small bungalow. Like many others on the same street, the house had been built in the town's heyday, the 1920s, before the Great Depression closed the nearby mines for many years.

World War II had brought back a measure of prosperity to the area, but it was short-lived. The flood was only the latest of many setbacks. Mac could see the despair on victim's faces, but he also saw gratitude and a glimmer of hope as more and more volunteers got to work.

He'd hardly had time to exchange a word with Jenny since he'd gone to her house, but she was in his mind whenever he had a moment to think. He was proud of her for organizing the youth to help in gathering supplies and spearheading their participation. One member of the group, Dave Phelps, came with his father to work on uprooted trees, cutting them into manageable logs with a chain saw.

He vetoed the idea of bringing the young people as a group until the more dangerous cleanup was done. Streets had to be cleared, and the Red Cross had to manage the effort to fight potential diseases. Everything exposed to the flood waters had to be sanitized. Even a child's tricycle had to be soaked in disinfectant for several hours in order to be reused. Trucks were filled with unsalvageable materials and goods as quickly as they arrived.

Mac forced himself to stop thinking of the plight of folks in the devastated town and put the finishing touches on his sermon. He felt bone weary. He'd gotten out of condition after his ankle injury, but he had to do something about it soon. Who knew what physical demands he might have to face in the future? And where?

This morning the church was as full as it had been on his first Sunday there, but Mac soon knew that his sermon was bombing. The amount of coughing, shuffling and throat clearing increased as he got into the heart of it. He looked down at Jenny sitting alone in the first pew, and she gave him a tiny nod of encouragement.

He knew what he had to do. He put aside his poorly written sermon and began talking from his heart, telling the congregation what they needed to hear.

"I pray that none of you will ever know how it feels to lose everything you have," he began.

People listened avidly while he first described the disaster in Dillard, then compared it to the grinding poverty he'd seen in his mission work.

"Am I my brother's keeper?" he asked. "The answer is a resounding yes."

He glanced at his watch and realized he'd talked way beyond his usual time. Then he looked at Jenny again and felt warmed by her smile.

He was overwhelmed by praise as people filed out after the service.

"Wonderful sermon," George Darlington said.

"Your best since you've been here," Minnie, his wife, added.

After thanking more people for their kind words, he looked around for Jenny. Had she ducked out the back way? He was beginning to wonder when almost everyone in attendance had greeted him on their way out. Finally she stepped in front of him.

"You did good," she said softly.

"I wrote a poor sermon," he admitted. "You're the one who encouraged me to forget it and just talk."

She only smiled. He had to wonder whether she was one of those rare people who were so attuned to others that they seemed to read minds. Or were they reaching out to each other in that mysterious way that his parents did?

"Can I see you later today?" he asked, lowering his voice, although it seemed no one else was close enough to hear.

"I think I might like that."

"Might?" He didn't know what he expected from her, but he liked that she smiled when she said it.

"Toby loves a stroller ride through Mason Park. He's always awake from his nap by three o'clock. Sometimes we see people we know there."

"I'm pretty sure you will today."

He was going to see Jenny. His heart was singing, and all the weariness of the past two weeks fell away.

Jenny hadn't realized how warm the day was until she started walking home from church. Damp tendrils of hair clung to her neck in the muggy heat, and one thing was certain. By afternoon it would be much too hot to take

Toby to the park. He didn't like his little cotton sun hat, and he got fussy when he was overheated. So much for her great idea of inviting Mac to join her in taking her nephew for a stroller ride.

When she got home, her mother was already involved in preparing Sunday dinner. It had been a family tradition for as long as Jenny could remember to have their big meal of the day after church. Her mother had insisted on continuing the noontime Sunday meal after her father left. It was her way of showing that they were still a close and loving family.

Fortunately it was a lighter meal than usual. Neither her sister nor her mother seemed to notice that she only picked at her serving of shrimp and macaroni salad. In fact, they both seemed to be preoccupied, and they could've been talking in code for all the sense Jenny made of their conversation.

When Toby went down for his nap, Jenny had to make a decision. Should she call Mac and tell him she wouldn't be at the park? She was at war with herself, good sense telling her to cancel their meeting but a stronger feeling overriding it. She wanted to be with him, even if it meant risking a world of hurt when he left Pleasantville.

Maybe he would stay. She wanted to believe it, but the town seemed too small for him. She'd seen how he came alive as he managed the church's response to Dillard's disaster. She didn't want to keep him from following a higher calling if that was the Lord's will. Now was the time to break things off between them for good.

The trouble was, her heart told her it was already too late.

Mac got to the park early and found it surprisingly quiet. A few people were enjoying the shaded walkways, and two elderly men were talking on one of the green slatted benches. The play equipment was nearly deserted though, no doubt because the community pool was more appealing on this hot afternoon. Mac had dressed for the weather in khaki walking shorts, a faded green T-shirt and a baseball cap that had seen service on two continents.

He felt conspicuous walking back and forth past the two old men, not wanting to go farther along the walking trail for fear of missing Jenny when she came—if she came. He was beginning to doubt that she would. He couldn't blame her for not taking Toby out in this heat, but he felt more and more disappointed as minutes ticked by on his watch. If she wasn't coming, why didn't she call? He had his cell phone in his pocket, and the number was included in every church bulletin in case a member of the congregation needed him in an emergency.

He found an empty bench and slumped down to brood, an unusual frame of mind for him. He was hanging around, hoping for a glimpse of Jenny, like an adolescent with his first crush.

It wasn't Jenny's fault that he couldn't get her out of his mind. She'd done little to encourage him. Quite the opposite, he had to admit. At first he'd thought she was too aloof. Now he recognized that she was only protecting herself from disappointment. He wasn't a great catch for any woman, despite what the matchmakers might think. The only certainty in his life was his determination to serve the Lord, but he still didn't know how or where he was to do that.

It was nearly three thirty. He could only assume that she wasn't coming. He stood up to leave and saw her approaching from the east, not the direction where he'd been expecting her. She'd been walking the trail that led away from the park and circled the town, a popular route for hikers and bikers.

"I'm sorry," she said a bit breathlessly. "I didn't realize how far I walked."

Her face was flushed even though she was wearing a cap with a bill. She was dressed all in white from her knit shirt to her walking shoes. He thought she'd never looked more beautiful, even with her upper lip beaded with moisture and her arms pink from the sun.

"I thought maybe you wouldn't come because it's too hot to walk Toby." He led the way back to the bench where he'd been so impatiently waiting.

"I wondered whether I should."

"I'm glad you did." It may have been the truest thing he'd ever said.

"There aren't many people here today."

She took off her hat and looked in both directions. Her honey-blond hair spilled loosely around her shoulders, and he was glad she hadn't experimented with it as some beauticians did, teasing it into unnatural spikes or dyeing it some bizarre color. In fact, Jenny was the most natural person he'd ever met. Her lack of artifice made her all the more appealing.

"We pretty much have the park to ourselves," he said.

The two elderly men were slowly strolling away without a backward glance.

"That's good. I mean, people are already gossiping about us. I'd much rather they didn't gossip anymore."

There were many things he wanted to say to her, but he didn't know how to begin. He wasn't even sure whether he should reveal any of his feelings. Despite the tenuous connection between them, they were still strangers, two people trying to work out their place in God's universe.

"I do want to thank you."

"For what?" She raised one eyebrow in a quizzical expression.

"For helping me save my sermon. I knew it was putting people to sleep. You encouraged me to toss it aside and say what I really wanted to."

"I did all that?" She laughed lightly. "I thought I was signaling you to cut it short."

"I got that message," he said laughing. "Maybe you could sit in the front pew every Sunday and give me a signal if I'm boring people."

"I wouldn't dream of it! You're usually right on target, although I wish you'd say something to let Harriet Hadley know that people like her even though they avoid her tuna curry casserole at potlucks."

They laughed together, and the tension he'd felt since first seeing her dissolved. They didn't have to work out their futures today. It was enough to enjoy her company, enough to be alone with her.

Her hand was resting on the bench beside him. He covered it with his, surprised at how delicate her fingers seemed and how soft her skin was. She didn't pull it away.

"It's a good day for doing nothing," he mused.

Hot as it was, there was no place he'd rather be than here in the park beside Jenny.

"You deserve some free time. I know how hard you worked in Dillard."

"You used all your days off to help too."

"Some of those houses were so bad that they needed a bulldozer to flatten them. By the way, I have an idea, maybe not a very good one, but I thought it might make some of the women feel a tiny bit better."

"What's that?"

"We're taking the youth group there at the end of the week, right?"

"I think they can be helpful by then without getting into any dangerous situations."

"I thought I'd set up to give free haircuts, maybe at the high school. Nothing lifts a woman's morale like a chance to look a little better."

He smiled at her and shook his head in wonderment.

"That's a great idea! One I would never have thought of. You're right on target, you know. The relief effort can repair physical damage to the town, but the trauma of having half the homes damaged or ruined by flood waters will be harder to get over."

"I thought maybe a couple of the girls could help me. You know, go out and urge people to come for a free cut, keep the floor swept, help with sanitizing combs and such."

"Only one problem," he said with mock seriousness.

"What?"

"I'll miss seeing you in those big boots you were wearing."

"I didn't know you saw me! I must have looked a fright."

"Not to me," he said softly, gently squeezing her hand.

"I'm glad you talked about Dillard in church. I've been proud of the way some people have come through, but there's a lot more our church could do."

She sounded a little breathless. Did she ignore his compliment because it made her uncomfortable? He had so much to learn about Jenny and not nearly enough time to do it. He took her hand and brushed his lips against her knuckles, wondering if it would take a lifetime to discover all the incredible things that made her who she was.

She pulled her hand away but didn't rebuke him. Still, his gesture put an end to their companionable time.

Moments later she made an excuse to hurry away. He watched her go, feeling more gloomy than ever about their chances of getting together.

Chapter Fourteen

As she approached Dillard, Jenny had serious reservations about what she was going to do there. Would people think she was foolish for offering haircuts when lives were in chaos? Only the encouragement Mac had given her kept Jenny from turning the car around and going home.

She had to give Charlene credit for rearranging the schedule at the shop to give her this day off. Not only that, her boss had loaned her a traveling kit, the supplies packed into a canvas bag that Charlene took to a nursing home once a month to do the ladies' hair there.

Three girls from the youth group were riding with her: Cindy, her cousin Madison who was visiting for a few weeks and Emily. They were excited about doing something to help the flood victims, and Jenny sincerely hoped that they'd take something positive from the experience.

The town looked a little better than it had last week, but Dillard was still in deep trouble. The only businesses open on Main Street were the pharmacy and the hardware store. The town's one supermarket had been packed with mud after the waters receded, and it wasn't certain whether the owners of the chain would ever reopen it.

"My dad said Dillard might become a ghost town," Cindy said. "He said there's nothing to keep people here."

"I don't know," Emily said. "If my family had lived here for hundreds of years, I would do anything I could to stay."

"It doesn't look like much of a town," Madison said, supporting her cousin.

"Oh, but it's such a pretty place to live—or it will be when everything is cleaned up," Emily said.

Jenny was happy to hear Emily debating with Cindy and her cousin. The youth group had done wonders to build her self-confidence.

As they arrived at the high school, they saw it had largely escaped flooding and now provided temporary housing for those who hadn't moved in with relatives or friends. The kitchen was serving three meals a day to both residents and volunteers, staffed by local church members and other helpers.

Jenny's trunk was full of food donations gathered by the young people, and more groceries were coming with Mac and church volunteers. Jenny was eager to set up her makeshift beauty parlor in the science lab, but first she helped the girls unload the food and wheel it to the kitchen on cafeteria carts.

The Red Cross was using the principal's office as a base of operations, and Jenny checked in there. Madge, the woman in charge, was a wonder of efficiency as she directed her team in controlling the filth and threat of diseases left behind by the floodwater.

"If I had time, I'd be your first customer," she told Jenny. "The quicker people go back to doing ordinary everyday things, the sooner they'll feel that they have their lives back."

Jenny appreciated her encouragement, but she was still afraid that no one would want to bother with something as mundane as a haircut. She hoped her helpers wouldn't be disappointed if no one came.

The science lab had long tables with stools for the students to do their experiments, but Jenny didn't see any seats that would work for a haircut. Cindy took the initiative and went to scour other classrooms for something suitable. She and Madison came back with a teacher's desk chair that adjusted to different heights. Jenny set up her equipment next to a sink and hoped at least a few people would take advantage of what she had to offer.

The three girls scattered to put up signs and left Jenny alone in the science lab. She idly studied a poster on the wall that showed the periodic table. She'd liked chemistry when she was in high school and still remembered many of the elements. Even though school had been out for at least a month, she still detected a trace odor of chemicals, a smell she'd never found unpleasant.

What would her life be like if she'd gone on to nursing school instead of training to be a beautician? She didn't regret her choice, but she was wondering more and more whether the future held more for her.

"Is it true what the girl said? You'll cut my hair for nothing?"

A haggard woman with sallow skin and dirty blond hair pulled severely back from her face stood in the doorway, as though not quite sure whether she should come in.

"I'd love to," Jenny said, relieved that at least one person wanted her services.

She whipped out a pretty pink cape and soon had the woman shampooed. The high faucet in the sink worked well, although the client had to stand over it instead of leaning back in a chair.

"Now, how would you like your hair cut?" she asked.

"Goodness, I don't know. I've never had a beauty parlor cut. My sister and I do each other's. Whatever you think will look good is fine with me."

Those words were a beautician's dream. Jenny studied the woman's rather long and bony face and decided on a layered cut that ended just below her jaw line. She set to work, delighted to be able to transform her.

Before she finished, a mother and daughter were waiting their turns, and several other people were hovering in the doorway, deciding whether to take advantage of the makeshift beauty parlor.

Whatever her three helpers were doing to attract attention, they were successful. People began flocking to the science lab, waiting patiently for a turn. One middle-aged woman in shabby jeans and a purple tunic volunteered to do shampoos. Jenny gratefully accepted her help. When Emily returned to see how things were going, Jenny put her to work sweeping up hair, sanitizing combs and generally helping out.

Noon hour came and went, marked only by a smell coming from the school kitchen that could have been spaghetti sauce. Every time Jenny finished one person, two others seemed to take her place. Some were so pleased with their new looks that Jenny had to fight back tears. She was doing so little, yet it seemed to mean so much to the women of Dillard.

Cindy and Madison returned and found ways to be helpful, until finally she insisted that the three girls go to the cafeteria and have some supper. Her shampoo lady had to leave, although she did so regretfully without having her own hair done, but there were still people waiting their turn.

Her arm ached, and she'd been standing on her feet far too long for comfort. She didn't know how she could keep styling hair at this pace, yet she continued, unwilling to turn anyone away. She was just finishing a round-faced teenager, fluffing out her cut with the dryer, when she heard the door close with a resounding bang. She didn't look around until her young client had profusely thanked her and was leaving.

The last person in the room wasn't there for a haircut. Mac smiled at her after he closed the door behind the girl.

"I think it's time to call it a day. Women all over town are looking pretty, thanks to you."

Jenny didn't know what to say. She was exhausted, but she'd never felt better about a day's work. When she thought about how grateful most of her clients had been, she felt downright weepy. Their lives had been devastated, but she'd been able to bring them a measure of happiness just by doing a small kindness.

"I saw a couple of our girls in the cafeteria," Mac said. "Why don't you come with me, and we'll check out what's for dinner?"

"I have to clean up here," she said.

"I'll help."

He swept the floor while she cleaned the sink and packed Charlene's traveling bag. It felt right and natural to be working with Mac, and he made the cleaning fun by joking and laughing. Some of her tiredness drained away, and she thanked the Lord that she'd been able to bring a tiny bit of happiness to the women of Dillard.

The school cafeteria was a big multipurpose room with tables that could be folded up and stored when they weren't needed. About half the places were occupied, but a few people were standing at the long service counter filling their trays with nourishing food prepared by volunteers.

"At night the tables go, and the room fills up with cots," Mac said. "At least the number of homeless has diminished quite a bit, but some have no place else to go until their homes are habitable again."

Jenny heard the sadness in his voice and fully shared his feelings. She better understood why mission work called to him, but she was going to miss him terribly when he was gone for good.

Cindy and the other girls were eating their dinner at a table with other young volunteers and seemed to be having a good time. Jenny followed Mac to the cafeteria line and picked up a tray still wet from the dishwasher.

Jenny was hungry enough to take a serving of everything, but the last thing she wanted to do was waste food when she had no idea how many others might come to be fed before the line closed for the evening. She settled for a small helping of macaroni and cheese and salad.

Mac led the way to an unoccupied table and unloaded both their trays, then went to get them something to drink. As he returned, she couldn't help but notice that his eyes were deeply shadowed. She'd never seen him looking so weary, and her heart went out to him. He was dressed in soiled jeans with a cell phone clipped to his belt and a black T-shirt that was ragged around the arms and ripped in several places. He didn't need to tell her that he'd been working with a cleanup team, doing the hard labor it took to clear away debris and begin home repairs where they were feasible.

"You look done in," she said.

"My batteries recharged when I saw you," he said, sitting across the table from her.

* * *

Mac was too tired to care about eating, but being with Jenny refreshed his soul. He speared a tomato from his salad, but he was too busy watching her to bring it to his mouth.

"Aren't you going to eat that?" she asked in a teasing voice.

"Oh, sure."

He wanted to tell her how beautiful she looked with her hair tumbling down her back and her cheeks flushed from working in a warm classroom. He wanted to tell her how he felt, but he didn't want to mislead her. How could he plan a future that included her?

"What made you want to be a beautician?" he asked conversationally.

"Originally, I wanted to be a nurse, but there was no money for school. Anyway, I've always enjoyed make-overs. When I was young, I used to give haircuts to my dolls. Once I even had the not-so-bright idea of using a felt pen as red dye. Unfortunately the ink was permanent, and one of my favorite dolls was transformed into a clown."

He laughed softly, so grateful to be sharing this meal with Jenny that he thanked the Lord for the opportunity.

"What did you like to do when you were a kid?" she asked, holding a bite of macaroni on her fork but not eating it.

"Explore. The first day I got a tricycle, I headed for the Pennsylvania border."

"The Pennsylvania border!"

"Actually, I only got as far as the next street over, but it was new territory to me."

"Your poor mother! You must have given her fits."

"I'm afraid I still do."

"She didn't like your mission work?"

"Her faith is too strong to deny that I had a calling, but I suspect that she prayed for me to come home the whole time I was gone."

"Do you have brothers or sisters?"

"No, but I have three redheaded cousins who loved to torment me whenever they visited. Now Sam is a doctor working in El Salvador, Vanessa works for a congressman in Washington and Chase is somewhere in South America. No one is quite sure what he's doing there."

"So wanderlust runs in your family."

"My mother blames it on Dad's Viking blood."

"You have a colorful family." At least she smiled when she said it.

"That's a kind way of putting it.

"How about your family?" he asked. "Do they have deep roots in West Virginia?"

"Dad never said much about it, and I never knew my grandparents on his side."

She spoke in a flat tone, but Mac read the pain behind her words. He could understand why she was so loyal to her remaining family. In fact, he suspected that her sister took advantage of it, putting a great deal of responsibility for Toby onto Jenny.

"How about your mother's side?"

"Oh, they've been here for ages. One ancestor fought in the Civil War, but Mom is a little vague about which side he was on. I've always thought it might be fun to find out more when I have time."

They ate in silence for a minute or two. Mac wanted to know all there was to know about Jenny, but he didn't want to pressure her.

"Can I get you some dessert?" he asked when they'd both made an attempt to finish their dinners.

"No, thank you. I'd better start for home. The girls' parents will be wondering where they are."

"I should go too. I let the Bible study ladies down last week. I'd better show up this week."

"I'm sure they understand the crisis here," she said.

"Yes, but I am their minister."

He was reminding himself, not Jenny. He might not be here long, but he fervently wanted to carry out his duties as faithfully as possible.

Jenny cleaned her place and went to round up the girls who'd ridden with her. As she left, Mac couldn't shake a deep feeling of sadness. His heart told him that there should be more between them, but his head rejected it.

He was caught unawares when Cindy and Emily, trailed by Cindy's cousin, ran over and gave him a hug.

"Thank you, Reverend Mac. I'm so glad I got to come here and help," Emily said.

"Me too!" Cindy said. "We never would've had this experience if you weren't our minister."

Mac was a little embarrassed by their enthusiastic thanks. When he looked up and saw Jenny watching, he was a lot embarrassed. She was grinning broadly, and he wondered if she'd put them up to it.

Chapter Fifteen

At the shop the next day, Charlene and Nadine were eager to hear all about her day in Dillard, but Jenny was at a loss for words to explain how it had made her feel.

"People were so grateful," she said, although that was only a superficial explanation for something that seemed life changing to her.

Even without their profuse thanks, she knew that she'd made some of the victims feel a little better. It was a different kind of giving than when she bought a new toy for Toby. She took pleasure in seeing him enjoy her gift, but she knew that it made no impact on his young life.

"Of course they were grateful," Charlene agreed. "I have to confess, I get more satisfaction from my trips to the nursing home than anything else I do."

Nadine was preparing her station before they opened for the day, but she stopped and gave them both a puzzled look.

"What about weddings?" she asked. "Think how happy you make the brides."

"They don't need my help to be happy on their wedding day," Charlene said philosophically. "If they do, maybe they shouldn't be tying the knot."

A brisk rapping sound got their attention. Their first client of the day was impatiently knocking on the front door, even though they weren't scheduled to open for another ten minutes. Jenny remembered the long lines of women patiently waiting their turn in Dillard and wished she were free to go back there today.

Kayla burst into the shop when Charlene unlocked the door.

"I know I don't have an appointment," she said breathlessly, "but I desperately need my hair styled. Can you possibly squeeze me in before your first appointment, Jenny?"

"What's the big event?" Charlene asked. She was always polite, but it annoyed her when anyone tried to get ahead of scheduled appointments.

"Oh, tonight's the Bible school picnic. I need a style that won't get all windblown."

"You didn't help with the program," Jenny said, wondering why her friend thought she should go.

"Actually I did. I helped my mother bake umpteen pans of cookies for the kids. If that doesn't make me a helper, I don't know what would."

"Jenny and I both have perms first thing this morning," Charlene said. "Maybe Nadine can help you."

"I have a half hour free for walk-ins," Nadine said, "if you don't want anything fancy."

"I thought Jenny…"

"Sorry, Jenny is booked solid this morning," Charlene firmly told her.

Jenny knew why Kayla was so eager to have her hair done for a church picnic. Her mother must have convinced her to get better acquainted with Mac. Jenny didn't want to be the one to burst her bubble, but she was positive that Mac wasn't looking for any kind of relationship during his brief stay in Pleasantville. The matchmakers, *even her own mother,* needed to cool it.

Mac wanted to be in Dillard, but his pastoral duties had piled up, leaving him little choice. He had to catch up on visitations, prepare an agenda for the church council meeting and generally take care of business. At least he'd set in motion a lot of volunteer help from his congregation.

This evening was the big fun fest for kids who'd attended summer Bible school. Besides a picnic supper, there would be games and activities, including the dreaded dunk tank. He'd volunteered—sort of—for a half-hour stint, sitting on a perch waiting for the hit that would plunge him into the water.

"Be sure to wear earplugs," Betty Jo said. "A few years ago George Darlington got an ear infection. Minnie won't let him do it anymore."

Mac smiled at his secretary, wondering how he'd get by without tapping into her font of information. No one, he was sure, knew more about the church and its members than she did.

"I'll have to get some," he said, his mind already racing on to the next thing he had to do.

"No, I'll do it before I go home for lunch. I need to pick up a prescription at the drugstore anyway. Call it my contribution to the picnic. I didn't get called to make cookies or anything."

Mac couldn't think of food without remembering supper with Jenny in the high school cafeteria. Had their time together meant as much to her as it did to him? How did she feel about him? Did she suspect he was falling in love with her? Women were supposed to have a sixth sense about things like that.

He slammed a desk drawer in frustration, then apologized to Betty Jo for startling her.

Why couldn't his life be less complicated? He was more committed than ever to serving the Lord and caring for others. Did that mean he should remain a solitary man, dedicated only to the church and his calling? Was there any place for Jenny in his life? Would it be fair to ask her to share his uncertain future?

Without realizing it, he sighed so deeply that his secretary noticed.

"Is there anything else I can do for you, Reverend Mac?" she asked.

"No thanks. I don't know what I'd do without your help, Betty Jo."

"If there's anything on your mind—"

"No, I'm just trying to figure out how to fit everything into my schedule."

Her smile looked suspiciously like a smirk. Was it possible she'd picked up on his interest in Jenny? If so, the whole congregation would be watching with eagle eyes to see whether it was true.

Should he throw caution to the wind and see Jenny wherever and whenever he wanted? He didn't mind if everyone in the world knew how special she was to him, but what would it do to Jenny? If he left to take a missionary post, everyone would think he'd dumped her. This town was her home. He didn't want her to be seen as an abandoned woman. He'd never felt so torn between what he thought was right and what he wanted to do.

Right now he wanted to ask her to come to the picnic. He couldn't face a whole day without seeing her.

Jenny walked home from work feeling as though her whole day had been wasted. Miss Dunning, the Sunday school superintendent, came in to have her roots touched up, but she adamantly refused to let Jenny restyle her fluffy blond hair. She was rail thin with rather poor posture, and a more modern hairstyle would've done a lot for her.

Mrs. Dodge, a widow in her late seventies, came for a perm. Jenny had tried to convince her to wait another month or two because her thinning hair needed more time to recoup. She wasn't successful there either. Mrs. Dodge was a dear, but she was lonely. She looked forward to lengthy hair appointments and the chance to gossip.

The Travis twins topped off her day. Jesse and Jason wiggled their way through haircuts like caterpillars on a hot grill. They were adorable from a safe distance, but she would be extremely grateful when they were old enough to go to the barbershop.

"Dear Lord," she silently prayed as she walked, "is this what I'm supposed to do with my life? Please show me the path that You would have me follow."

When she got home, Toby was in his playpen in the front room. It wasn't his favorite place, and he'd protested by throwing his toys over the bars. Jenny wondered how long it would be before he learned how to go over the top himself.

"Hi, sweetie," she said scooping him up and carrying him to the kitchen where she expected her mother to be preparing dinner. They took turns, and Tuesday was always her mother's day.

"Mom?"

Toby was kicking and squirming, wanting to be let

down. She put him on the floor and followed as he crawled toward the bedrooms at the rear of the house.

Gloria was in her bedroom, putting the finishing touches on her upswept hair. She didn't look like a mother about to prepare dinner. In fact, Jenny noticed that she was wearing one of her best summer dresses, a pretty lavender-and-blue print.

"Oh, there you are, dear," she said. "How was your day?"

"Fine."

Her mother had asked the same question every day for more years than Jenny could remember. She always gave the same answer. Her mother genuinely cared, but a negative answer would upset her. Sometimes Jenny felt that their roles had somehow become reversed, that she was the one who had to take care of her only parent.

"I hope you don't mind if I don't cook tonight. There's a pizza in the freezer you can heat up."

"I'll be fine, but where are you going?"

"You might say I have an appointment for dinner."

"A date?"

"Well, yes, you could put it that way." Gloria's cheeks were flushed, and she didn't look directly at her daughter.

"With a man?" Jenny was stunned. She'd never imagined her mother dating.

"Well, yes, of course with a man," she said a bit impatiently. "Mature adults do enjoy each other's company on occasion."

"I'm happy for you," Jenny was quick to say. "You just surprised me."

"Well, I'm a little surprised myself. I've known George Hunter for ages, long before he married that woman from New Jersey. They're divorced, you know. Have been for years. She left him for someone else. We just happened to meet in the produce department of the supermarket. We started talking, and well, here I am, getting all dressed up to go to out to dinner. We may take in a movie, too, so don't wait up for me, dear."

"I hope you have a nice time," Jenny said.

She scooped up Toby, guessing that he'd had his dinner because his shirt had fresh orange and green stains.

"Let's see what your mother is up to," she said, carrying him across the hall to Sandy's room.

The door was open, but her sister wasn't there. Jenny put her nephew down on the floor and watched as he explored his mother's room. She didn't have to wait long. Sandy came through the door in her terry cloth bathrobe, her hair wrapped in a towel.

"Oh, good, you're home. Can I ask a huge favor? I thought Mom could watch Toby tonight, but she has plans. Would you mind terribly?"

"I guess not. Where are you going?"

"I'm not sure."

"That's not an answer. You have to tell the babysitter where you'll be."

"You know my cell phone number."

Jenny folded her arms across her chest and didn't say anything.

"All right, you'll find out soon enough anyway. I have a date."

What was happening to her family? All of a sudden her mother and her sister were dating.

"Is it anyone I know?"

"I doubt it. His name is Luke Barrington. He's the new football coach at the high school. He'll be teaching math too."

"Where did you meet him?"

"You won't believe this. I went to Reverend Mac's support group, and he was there. His parents were both killed in a car crash last year, and he's still working his way through the grief process. He made my problems with Duane seem pretty insignificant."

Jenny was beginning to wonder whether she'd come home to the wrong house, but Toby assured her she hadn't when he tipped over his mother's wastebasket and started chewing on a tissue. Sandy retrieved him and gave her a beseeching look.

"Would you mind terribly? Luke will be here any minute."

"Come on, Toby. You and I have a date tonight," Jenny said, feeling disgruntled over once again being the designated babysitter.

She adored her nephew, but Sandy was making a habit of assuming Jenny would watch him. And how was it possible that both her mother and her sister had dates? Life seemed to be passing her by. Would she end up the old-maid aunt who could always be relied on to watch other people's children?

She put him in the playpen for a minute and tossed in some toys. She wanted to change out of the warm slacks she'd worn to work, but before she could go to her own room, the phone rang.

She took it in the kitchen.

"Jenny, this is Mac…Arnett."

"Actually you're the only Mac I know," she teased.

"I know this is last minute, but I didn't want to call you at work."

"What's last minute?"

"How would you like to watch while people throw baseballs and dunk me in a water tank?"

"That's happening tonight, isn't it? The Bible school picnic."

"It won't hurt my feelings if you throw a few too."

"You're asking me to go? I didn't help with the kids this year."

"I guess that would make me your date."

She looked through the door at Toby who was in the process of throwing out his toys again.

"I'm babysitting my nephew."

"It's never too late to acquaint him with church activities," he suggested.

It was a crazy idea, taking Toby to the picnic, but she really wanted to go. She realized that her day had seemed empty and pointless because she hadn't seen Mac.

"He likes watching people, especially other kids. I guess I could give it a try. If he gets too fussy, I can always bring him home."

"That's great!"

Ten minutes later she had Toby buckled into his car seat with a loaded diaper bag and stroller in the trunk of the car. She was nervous, but not because she was worried about what the people there would think. She just wanted to see Mac so badly that nothing about her seemed right. She didn't have time to shower and do her hair. Her denim skirt and pink knit shirt made her feel shabby compared to her mother and sister. She was afraid she'd get there and he wouldn't pay any attention to her. But of course he would, and she knew that this was a big step forward in their relationship. It was a public declaration that they were interested in each other, but where would it lead?

When she got to the park, the picnic was in full swing. One of the teachers was grilling hot dogs, a sack race was in progress and the younger children were enjoying the play equipment. The center of attention was the dunking machine, rented every year for the event. Mac was having his turn, although he wasn't the first target. Dave Phelps was standing nearby, soaking wet with a towel around his head.

She pushed the stroller as close as she could to the dunk tank and watched as two middle-school boys took turns throwing the baseballs. One missed the target and the other didn't throw hard enough to propel Mac into the water.

Mac looked in her direction and smiled.

Jenny had come. He didn't notice when Dave stepped up to take a turn at throwing, but he felt the thud as his ball connected with the target. An instant later he was in the water, soaked from head to feet, scrambling back up to his perch to await the next plunge.

He went into the tank three more times, which probably wasn't a bad average considering that everyone thought it was hilarious to dunk the preacher. When his turn was over, he dried off as best he could with a big towel Betty Jo had provided for the event. He didn't even think of going home to shed his wet jeans and shirt. Jenny was waiting for him.

"What is it with you and water?" she teased.

He took out the earplugs Betty Jo had provided and stuffed them into his pocket.

"The next time I get this wet, I want to be swimming in a pool." He smiled at Jenny.

"Hi, Toby," he said, bending down and taking the tiny hand in his. "Really glad you could make it."

"He's really happy to be here."

Toby stared at the crowd around him, totally indifferent to Mac and Jenny. She started pushing his stroller toward the play equipment, but it was hard going on the grass. Mac took over for her, but he didn't get far. Kayla had stepped in front of the stroller, blocking his progress.

"Reverend Mac, you are such a good sport to sit there letting people dunk you," she said.

"Thank you," he said, trying to shrug off her compliment and continue pushing Toby.

"I don't care much for hot dogs, so my mother packed a picnic lunch for me. There's more than enough for two if you'd like to share it."

"That's nice of you, Kayla. Thank you, but I think Jenny and I will just grab a hot dog."

"Oh." Kayla looked at Jenny, and her expression changed. "You really should have told me you were coming."

"It was a last-minute arrangement. Reverend Mac and I are just friends."

Jenny knew that Kayla was hurt because she hadn't confided in her. They'd always shared everything in their lives, but Kayla hadn't had a clue that she was interested in Mac. Her friend hated to be out of the loop, especially since she'd seen her that morning.

"Well, have fun," Kayla said, quickly leaving them.

"Is it true that we're only friends?" Mac asked softly.

"How else could I explain being here with you?"

"I guess you couldn't tell Kayla that I can't seem to stay away from you."

"Can't you? You have a funny way of showing it. Sometimes I don't hear from you for days on end."

"Not because I don't want to see you."

"No, you're busy, and you don't want to get involved because you can't wait to get back to some jungle village where people will really appreciate you."

"That's a harsh way to put it." He managed to sound angry and upset without raising his voice.

"It's true, isn't it? We're not friends because friends let each other know what they're feeling. How do you feel about me, Mac?"

"Jenny, I care about you a great deal."

"Care! That's a convenient generic word. I care about Pleasantville. I care about my family. I care about keeping our bird feeder stocked in the winter."

"You know what I feel goes beyond birdseed."

Now she knew how he looked when he was angry. His brows came together and his lips formed a tight line. At least she was getting an honest reaction from him.

"I don't know anything! I have no idea what I want to do with the rest of my life, but I'm pretty sure it won't be the same routine, day after day, until I'm too old to lift a pair of scissors." She surprised herself by spouting off this way, but her feelings for Mac were so bottled up that she felt like exploding.

"If you're unhappy with your life—"

"I'm not unhappy! I'm perfectly happy. Don't you dare try to counsel me."

"You don't have to get angry."

"I'm not angry. I'm just…"

As if on cue, Toby started howling. Mac picked him up, but it was past his bedtime. He was beyond comforting.

"I have to take him home now," she said, lifting him away from Mac.

"I'll come with you."

"No, we don't have anything else to say to each other."

She didn't let Mac push the stroller to her car. When she looked back, Miss Dunning and two mothers had cornered him.

Jenny was sure of one thing: a minister was just an ordinary man who could make mistakes and get angry. She was going to work very hard to get him out of her mind. They had nothing in common, and she didn't want to pin any hopes on him.

The matchmakers were welcome to use every trick in the book to ensnare him. If and when she decided to change her life, it wouldn't have anything to do with Mac.

"We're going home, Toby," she said as she struggled to put him in his car seat. "You're my main man, and I adore you, but I have a life to lead. Mommy had better stop assuming I'm always available to babysit."

That was the solution to the rut she was in. She was going to start dating, never mind that the prospects weren't promising. She had to get out more. It might not be a solution, but it was a place to start.

Chapter Sixteen

Jenny didn't wait up for her mother and sister to get home, but lying in bed didn't mean she was sleeping. It wasn't surprising that she'd been attracted to Mac. He'd traveled as she'd always dreamed of doing. He was a committed Christian, making her want to strengthen her own faith. And, she had to admit, he was handsome, outgoing and appealing in every way. He also didn't have enough sense to see that they belonged together.

There were no promises between them, no shared goals and no spoken vows. Sometimes he made her heart beat fast and her pulse race. Other times she felt rejected and more alone than ever before. She'd made the right decision: she needed a better social life. Bring on the blind dates!

Eventually she fell asleep, but she awoke in the morning feeling listless and tired. Her big solution didn't seem nearly as appealing as it had in the small hours of the night.

Sandy and her mother were chatting over cereal and coffee at the breakfast table when Jenny came into the kitchen.

"How did your big evenings go?" she asked, wanting to focus the conversation on them. Even Sandy was likely to notice how haggard she looked.

"George is such a lovely man," her mother said. "I can't wait to have you meet him. I invited him to dinner Saturday. I hope both of you can be there."

"Sure, Mom," Jenny said, mildly curious about her mother's friend and happy that she had a new interest.

"Brilliant idea!" Sandy said, getting up from the table. "Why don't I invite Luke? I bet he could bring a friend for you, Jenny."

"No!" Jenny said adamantly. "Don't you dare try to fix me up with anyone, Sandra Marie!"

She hadn't changed her mind about starting to date again, but her sister was the last person she'd trust as a matchmaker. Before she separated from Duane, she'd tried too many times to foist his unappealing cousins on her.

"You don't have to be hostile," Sandy said in her most annoying big-sister tone. "I just thought it would be nice to have even numbers. If you want to invite someone on your own, that's fine."

"Sandy is right," their mother agreed. "Even numbers would be nice. Do you think we should grill outside? Or maybe I should make beef Stroganoff. What do you think, Jenny?"

"Everything you make is good."

"I still think it would be a good idea to have Luke bring a friend for you," Sandy persisted.

Jenny poured herself a small glass of orange juice and hurriedly drank it. She did not want to have this conversation, not this morning or ever. She was still getting used to her mother and her sister having boyfriends. She hated the idea that Sandy would drag someone to the house to meet her. How could she trust her taste in men? After all, she'd married a man who had "loser" written all over him.

"If you want me to be there, don't use it as a blind date opportunity," Jenny said. "I'm off to work."

"So early?" Gloria asked.

"Busy day. I'll see you tonight."

Mac used the church directory to plan his visitations, listing people by neighborhood or area rather than alphabetically. His father always stressed how important it was for a minister to get to know his flock. There was no substitute for sitting down in a person's home and having a quiet talk.

Like his father, he was making his visits without calling ahead. He didn't want people baking cookies, cleaning house, or generally putting themselves out on his account.

Retirees were easy to find at home, but it was harder to time his visits to working people. Betty Jo helped him by pointing out those who worked night shifts. He had the youth group tonight, but he thought he could squeeze in a few stops in the late afternoon.

It wasn't coincidence that just before the dinner hour he found himself in the neighborhood of modest frame houses where Jenny lived. He parked his car at the end of her block and looked in on the Harburg family. They didn't attend church regularly and were a bit embarrassed by his unexpected call. Mac was quick to put them at ease, assuring them that the church would welcome them with open arms whenever they felt moved to come.

He didn't linger after he accomplished his purpose, but he did sit in his car afterward, wondering whether he should make Jenny's house his next destination. There were a lot of reasons not to call on her family. He hadn't parted on cordial terms with Jenny, and a pastoral call might make things worse because she'd certainly see through his excuse for coming.

While he debated with himself, he saw Jenny walking toward her house and going up to the door.

He didn't know whether she would be alone, but he made up his mind. He wanted to see her, no matter what the circumstances.

Rather than drive the short distance, he left the car and walked to her house, knocking softly on the door. She answered almost immediately.

She hadn't changed out of the dark slacks and pink knit top she wore as a uniform to work, but her hair was hanging free, sweeping down beside her luminous hazel eyes and framing her lovely face. If she was surprised to see him, she didn't show it.

"Mac."

"I was out making visitations, and I saw you come home. I'll only stay a minute."

"Come in. My sister and mom aren't home yet. One or the other of them has to pick up Toby at day care."

She motioned for him to sit on the floral-patterned couch in the living room and took a seat across the room from him on a pale gold wing chair. The room was done in muted shades of green, gray and yellow, a peaceful setting although it showed signs of age. Toby's playpen filled the space at one end, and his toys were stacked on the coffee table in front of him. He felt at home even though he wasn't at ease about his reason for being there.

"We have youth group tonight," he said, stating the obvious.

"Yes."

"That's not why I'm here."

"Oh?"

"Is there any way we can be more than friends?" He was asking himself as much as Jenny.

"I don't know."

What did he expect her to say? He hadn't given her any reason to expect more from him, but his heart ached to tell her how he really felt.

"I've given you the wrong impression. I like my job here. The flood in Dillard made me realize how great the needs in this state are. But that doesn't mean I'll be asked to stay on. There's still a strong chance that I'll be leaving when my year is up. Then…" He shrugged. "I just don't know."

"I understand. It's your career."

Her tone told him more than her words. She thought his calling as a minister would always come before personal feelings. Maybe it was true, but he wanted her to know that there was room in his life for both. First, though, he wanted her to understand what his calling meant to him.

"I often felt inadequate in my mission assignments. People were suffering from starvation and disease, and I'm not a doctor. The poverty I saw was overwhelming, but I didn't have the financial resources to change lives. I talked to people about a compassionate Lord, but sometimes the misery of innocent children tested my faith. I couldn't stop war, famine or disease, and it ate away at me."

When she didn't say anything, he added, "I just wanted you to know."

Jenny felt off balance, not sure what Mac expected her to say. Why had he come? Did he have any idea how important he'd become to her?

"Whatever you think, you're the best friend I have," he said in a muted voice.

She wanted to protest. How could he think of her as only a friend when she longed to be part of his life, no matter where he went or what he did? But was she strong enough to be his helpmate? While he was struggling with big, important issues, she was focused on the emptiness in her own life. Did that make her unworthy of a man like him? The terrible thing was, the more she understood his life, the less she felt worthy of sharing it.

"I appreciate what you're saying." But she still didn't know where this conversation was leading.

"I'm saying that I love you."

She drew in a deep breath, feeling as though her lungs had deflated like popped balloons.

"I—"

Before she could react, the front door opened.

"Gaga," Toby gurgled as he crawled toward her, followed by both her mother and sister.

Jenny scooped him up for a hug, but she was dismayed by their timing. Mac stood up to greet them, but he didn't sound like his usual outgoing self.

"What a nice surprise to see you here," her mother was quick to say.

"Mac and I were talking about an idea Charlene had," she improvised, dredging up a possibility they'd tossed around at work today. "The shop usually closes Saturday afternoon, but she's willing to stay open for a special event. We thought people could either bring canned goods or donate money in exchange for hairstyling. It looks like Dillard will need help for quite a while."

"It's a great idea," Mac said.

"We're going to talk about fundraising ideas with the youth group this evening," she said, talking too fast and not looking at Mac.

"I may be a little late," he said. "I have more calls to make."

"No problem," Jenny said, trying to ignore her racing pulse. Mac said he loved her! She couldn't quite believe she'd heard him right.

"Well, I should be going." He bent and patted Toby's head.

As Mac was leaving, she thought of the dinner party her mother and sister were planning. She very much wanted to invite him, but her mother was one step ahead of her. Before he made it to the door, Gloria asked him to come. For once her matchmaking ways were right on target, but Jenny couldn't tell her that.

She had no idea what would happen next. Maybe Mac meant to say that he loved her but couldn't make any commitments. Maybe this was the beginning of the end, not a step forward in their relationship. How could she possibly wait until after the meeting tonight to find out?

Was it possible for a man and a woman to be friends after they'd fallen in love?

Mac skipped dinner and managed to get through his quota of calls in less time than he'd anticipated. He felt good about his ministerial calls. Each one he made brought him closer to members of his congregation and more in tune with their needs.

Now that his visitations were over for the day, he couldn't get back to the church fast enough. The youth meeting would be well underway, and he didn't want Jenny to go home until he got there.

The more he saw her, thought about her and daydreamed about her, the more important it seemed to go forward with their relationship. He'd told her he loved her, but they'd been interrupted before she could react. He didn't know where to go from there when his own future was so unsettled, but he desperately wanted to know how Jenny felt about him.

Jenny couldn't have been more pleased with the young people in the church. The meeting was going great, but she checked her watch every few minutes, wondering whether Mac would get there before it was over. If he didn't, should she wait at the church? She still found it hard to believe, but he'd told her that he loved her. She couldn't wait to see him again.

When Mac finally got there, the meeting was over. He came back into the meeting room while she was straightening chairs to avoid leaving.

"Did it go well?" he asked, but she could tell his mind wasn't on the youth group.

"Yes." She straightened another chair although it wasn't out of place.

"I got back as soon as I could."

"I know how busy you must be."

"Every family I visit seems to have a problem or an issue to discuss, but that's not a bad thing. I guess it shows I really am needed here."

She thought of the women lining up for haircuts in Dillard and understood something of what he meant. She would've loved to unburden herself and put her troubles on his broad shoulders, but this wasn't the time or the place.

"My sister has gotten a lot out of your support group," she said. "In fact, she's started dating one of the other members."

"That's great! I don't deserve the credit, though. Sandy

was ready to move on. She realized it herself when she had a chance to speak out to a sympathetic group."

"I've had another surprise this week. My mother has reconnected with an old friend. It's the first time she's dated since my dad left. It's hard to take in, so much happening at once."

"I couldn't be happier for your family. Your mother and sister deserve a fresh start." He smiled down at her, and she felt love radiating from him.

This was no time to be coy. "About what you said—"

"That I love you."

"I feel the same way."

Her words came out in a soft whisper but when he took her in his arms, there was no question that he'd heard.

"What are we going to do about us?" he whispered into her hair.

She didn't have answers, but for the moment it was enough to be with him.

Later, when he left her at her door, everything between them had changed but nothing was resolved. He didn't say it, but she knew there was no place for her in his life if he took a foreign missionary assignment. What could she possibly contribute to his work?

She imagined herself in a remote village devastated by mudslides or war or famine, offering the ladies a free haircut. If she didn't feel so inadequate, she would have laughed at the idea. What could she possibly do to be a worthy partner for Mac?

Chapter Seventeen

Jenny decided to be discreet with her mother and sister. If they knew how much she and Mac cared for each other, they'd start planning a wedding. Their disappointment would be one more burden she'd have to carry when he left.

At least she had a partner for their dinner. Sandy could stop pressuring her. Anyway, her sister had her hands full trying to find a sitter for Toby. She and Gloria had agreed to make this an adults-only meal, especially because Toby tended to be cranky after his own dinner. Finally Jenny stepped in and arranged for Nadine to watch him at her parents' house for a few hours Saturday evening.

"I'm lonely anyway since Clark went into the military," she said when Jenny asked her. "If this town had any decent jobs, he would've stayed here. We want to get married, but that's on hold now."

She'd recently dyed her hair a bright pink, but it did nothing to make her look more cheerful since her boyfriend had left.

Jenny's heart went out to her. Pleasantville was a nice

town in a lovely setting, but the young men drifted away in alarming numbers. There just weren't enough opportunities.

It was beginning to seem unlikely that Mac would be offered a permanent position. She'd heard rumors— rather, her mother had—that the church leaders liked the way he was doing his job but still preferred an older, more settled man. In other words, they wanted a married man with a family, someone who would have a greater stake in the community.

Jenny didn't know how she felt about the dinner. Certainly she was curious to meet the men who'd come into her mother and sister's lives, but she could be making a mistake by having Mac come. Mom and Sandy would sense that there was something new between them. She didn't know how she could look at him without giving away her feelings. She never had been able to disguise how she felt and she felt overwhelmed by his love for her and hers for him.

She desperately wanted to see him—alone.

Mac hadn't had a chance to see Jenny since the youth group meeting, but they'd talked on the phone late every evening. She was never far from his thoughts, and the time was coming when he had to make a decision.

He didn't question how he felt about Jenny. This was definitely love, but the obstacles remained the same. Where would he be a year from now? Could he ask her to share his life when he didn't know where the Lord would have him go next?

He prayed for guidance. A telephone call came late Friday afternoon.

"We don't want you to make a decision right now," the head of the mission board assured him. "We know you have an obligation to finish your interim year, but you should know that we'll have an overseas position for you when you're ready."

When he came back to the States for his ankle surgery, Mac had worried that his usefulness to the poor and suffering in third world countries was over. This was the reassurance he'd needed then, but now he didn't know how he felt about it. Alone, he wouldn't hesitate to go places where disease and political upheaval made every day a dangerous challenge, but he loved Jenny too much to risk her health and safety. Nor was it likely that he would be allowed to take an untrained person into the kind of situation that sometimes faced the church's missionaries.

Was the Lord testing his faith? Did he have to give up the things he wanted most in life, a loving wife and family, to serve Him?

He wanted to talk to his father but suspected that he was as eager to see him settled with children of his own as his mother was. Jenny was the only one who would really understand, but as soon as he told her about the offer, he would have to make his decision. He couldn't leave her hanging, not knowing whether they had a future together.

For now, he could only pray for guidance. Tomorrow he would have to sit down for a meal with Jenny and her family. He was sure their feelings for each other wouldn't be a secret after that. It was hard enough explaining his situation to the woman he loved. Her family might never understand.

Five minutes before the men were expected, everyone was ready. The food was in the kitchen, the roast was waiting in a warm oven, the house was as close to immaculate as possible and Toby's playpen and toys were out of sight in his room.

Jenny felt like plain Jane next to her mother and sister. Both of them had dug deep into their closets for party wear. Mom was wearing a lavender print silk jacket over a yellow dress. Sandy sparkled in a sequin-trimmed pink bridesmaid's dress that she'd shortened herself. Jenny had settled for light blue slacks and a white crinkle cloth tunic. She wished they weren't making such a big deal of the dinner, but she was the first to admit that both of them needed more fun in their lives.

Her real concern was how her family would overreact when they realized that things were serious between Mac and her, serious but unresolved. Still, she was so eager to see him that her heart skipped a beat when the doorbell rang.

George Hunter, her mother's friend, was the first to arrive. He was a man of average height, slender and a bit stoop-shouldered. He had an ample amount of silver hair brushed back from a rather high forehead and light blue eyes that looked at her mother with fondness and approval. He'd obviously gone to some trouble to present himself well. His light beige summer suit was meticulously pressed, and he wore a color-coordinated shirt and a conservative tie in shades of mocha and cocoa.

"These are for you," he said, handing Gloria a bouquet of sunny yellow, white and orange flowers.

Jenny could tell her mother was thrilled. She immediately had a good opinion of George, not because of the flowers but because he looked at Gloria with adoring eyes. Her mother looked young and pretty again under his gaze.

As soon as George settled down on the couch in front of a tray of appetizers the doorbell rang again. Sandy correctly guessed that it was Luke and met him at the door.

"Everyone, this is Luke," she said, introducing him to the others in the room.

George stood to shake his hand, an act of courage because the football coach had bear-size paws that literally engulfed the older man's. He had the height to match his hands, standing at least six foot four with brown hair cut close to his scalp and dark eyes that focused on Sandy even as he met the others. He'd made an effort to dress for dinner, his broad shoulders straining against the fabric of a wool houndstooth sports jacket that must have been uncomfortable on the warm summer day.

"Something smells good," Luke said, even though Jenny was pretty sure the aroma of the roast didn't carry to the living room.

She suspected he'd rehearsed the line ahead of time to have something to say. He hovered close to Sandy and accepted a plate of appetizers she prepared for him, eating them as he stood. He was good-looking in a rugged, athletic way, but he seemed uncomfortable with the small talk in the room. If he was serious about Sandy, he was probably intimidated by his first meeting with her family. Jenny asked him a few questions about his move to Pleasantville and his new job to put him at ease. He seemed grateful for her effort to pull him into the conversation.

Mac was late. Maybe he had an emergency, a sudden illness or death in the congregation. Or maybe he just had reservations about coming. The conversation was flowing around her now, but she scarcely followed it as she waited for him to arrive. Then there was a soft rap on the front door. It had to be Mac.

"I'll get it," she said, although no one else made any move to do so.

"Sorry I'm late," Mac said, standing on the threshold in a dark suit, crisp white shirt and red patterned tie. He didn't offer any explanation for his tardiness, but she was too glad to see him to care.

He greeted George and Luke like old friends and complimented both her mother and sister on how nice they looked. He brought something more important than flowers into the room. His easy conversation and outgoing nature soon had everyone talking as if they'd known each other for years. It was impossible for anyone to be stiff or awkward around Mac. He genuinely liked people, and the good will he brought with him made everyone relax, everyone except Jenny.

He didn't ignore her. He just didn't focus on her the way George and Luke did with her mother and sister. She was grateful that they weren't the center of attention. They were halfway through the dinner, enjoying the roast that George had carved with suitable ceremony, before Mac reached under her great-grandmother's linen cutwork tablecloth and gently squeezed her hand. He pulled away a moment later to pass the bowl of parsley potatoes and onions to Luke, whose appetite matched his size, but her fingers felt warm and tingly long after his hand was gone.

George was especially interested in Mac's experiences as a missionary. He'd done a stint in the Peace Corps when he was young, and they seemed to have a lot in common. As dinner parties went, this one was a big success.

Jenny was happy for her mother and sister's sake, but their happiness only highlighted the uncertain status of her relationship with Mac.

After dessert, George insisted the young people leave the kitchen work to him. He helped Gloria clear the table, then the two of them tackled the dishes.

"I hate to leave you two alone," Sandy said to her sister, "but I have to pick up Toby at the sitter's. Luke is going to drive me there so he can see Toby before he goes to bed."

Jenny found herself alone in the living room with Mac, but she felt the constraint between them. He'd been talkative during the meal, but now he seemed hesitant to say what was on his mind.

"Would you like to take a walk before it rains?" he asked.

"Rain?" she asked. "It's been nice all day."

"My ankle has a built-in storm gauge. I think the surgeons must have sewed in a barometer, but we should have an hour or two before the rains come."

She laughed, but it was a bit forced.

"All right," she said. "Should I take an umbrella?"

"No, I'm sure we'll be back in time."

She could hear the rattle of dishes in the kitchen. Her mother would probably appreciate being left alone with George.

"Let's go then."

Mac wasn't sure how to tell Jenny about the phone call from the head of the mission board, but he prayed for inspiration as they began walking through her neighborhood. He hadn't been kidding about his ankle, but that wasn't what concerned him. He couldn't keep seeing her without telling her where he stood in his career.

"I had a phone call this afternoon," he slowly began.

"Anything important?"

"Yes and no."

He knew it was a dumb answer, but he didn't know how he felt about going back into the mission field, let alone how to tell her about the offer.

"If you don't want to tell me—"

"I do. The call was from the head of the mission board, my former boss."

"Oh."

He heard the dread in her voice and knew he couldn't prolong this.

"He offered me a foreign posting when my year here is over."

"You're leaving for sure then?" Her voice was so low he had to strain to hear.

"No! I mean, I haven't made any decision. I don't even know whether the church here will offer me a permanent position." He was botching this, but he desperately wanted to be completely honest with her. "Right now, I'm in limbo. I want to serve the Lord as best I can, but I don't know where that will lead me."

"I see."

He didn't think she did.

"Jenny, I don't want to leave you."

He spoke from the depths of his heart, but he didn't feel free to go beyond that. What could he promise her? He didn't know what the future held, let alone where he would be in less than a year.

She walked with her eyes on the ground, not saying anything.

"You mean a lot to me, Jenny."

He wanted to reassure her that he loved her, but wouldn't that make his indecision seem worse, not better?

"I just want you to know where I stand," he said.

Everything he said made things worse between them. He wanted to take her in his arms and promise never to leave her, but he might not be given a choice. If the Bible Church didn't extend his one-year contract, he didn't know how he could refuse a mission call.

"Serving the Lord will always be your first priority. I know that, Mac. I wouldn't expect any less from you."

Her words were meant to comfort, but he felt as though his heart were being torn apart. Most ministers married and had families. His own mother had supported his father throughout his years of service to the church, but the senior Reverend Arnett had never been called to foreign missions. He hadn't experienced the grinding poverty in places like Haiti and East Africa.

He smiled ironically at the thought of his mother in the Haitian mountain settlement where his group had labored to build a church and bring the Word to people the world had forgotten. His fledgling congregation there was crippled by preventable diseases and plagued by a poor diet and lack of plumbing and a safe water supply. His mother would be horrified by a situation like that.

He suspected that Jenny had more grit than his genteel mother, but he didn't want her subjected to unhealthy conditions, political upheaval and the threat of danger. His own mission experiences had tested his faith and made him angry at the suffering of the poor. Once, he'd been felled by disease, lying in a primitive hut unable to lift his head, hoping a shipment of antibiotics would get through in time to save him. His broken ankle, left untreated too long, was going to bother him for the rest of his life, but it was a small annoyance compared to what poverty-stricken people endured in countless countries.

"I should go home now," Jenny said, breaking into his tortured thoughts. "You're right. It does look like rain."

"Jenny…"

There were a thousand things he wanted to say to her. In his eyes she was the most beautiful woman in the world. He loved her kindness and generosity, her gentle ways with people and her willingness to step forward wherever she was needed. She deserved the best that life had to offer, but all he had brought to her was heartache. He knew how she felt about him. He could read it in her eyes and hear it in her voice when they were alone. He was hurting her by his inability to make plans for a future together.

He didn't know why the Lord had brought him to West Virginia, but he prayed that he wouldn't hurt Jenny too badly if he had to leave. For now, he couldn't think of anything else to say to her.

"You're right. We should go back," he said.

In her heart Jenny was sure Mac loved her, but she just didn't fit into his life. He was meant to do the Lord's work in ways she couldn't fathom. She would be a liability. The best thing she could do for him was to back away graciously and show that she understood why they couldn't be together. But was she strong enough to do that?

Her mother and George were quietly talking in the living room when she got back. She told her mother's friend how pleased she was to meet him, then went toward her room.

Toby's door was open and his crib was empty. Her sister hadn't returned yet. For a moment she envied her. She'd found a decent man with a job in Pleasantville. Whatever happened between them, they wouldn't have to face the obstacles she and Mac did. But in her heart, she knew Sandy had been hurt by Duane's betrayal and deserved another chance at happiness. She prayed she wouldn't be hurt again.

When she was alone in her room, Jenny's first instinct was to cry, but tears weren't going to help anything. For the first time in her life, she was truly and deeply in love. How many times would that happen? Look how long her mother had waited to forge a new relationship with a man.

Jenny wanted more from life, but not because she was discontented with what she had. She just felt sure that she had more to give and more to experience. The question was, what could she do to put her life on a different path? And what could she do to be part of Mac's?

Chapter Eighteen

Mac almost wished he hadn't picked up a copy of the weekly *Pleasantville Herald* on his way to the church on Saturday morning. The news from towns hit hardest by the flood wasn't good. Several were suffering from severe water shortages after the municipal supply was contaminated. It was going to take months, if not years, to repair or replace all the damaged homes and commercial buildings.

What could one man do to help? Not much, he knew, but with faith in the Lord and the support of a willing congregation, he could make a difference. He had to believe that.

The past week had been the most discouraging of his ministry to date, but it wasn't just the overwhelming needs of stricken communities that troubled him. He hadn't seen Jenny since the dinner at her house last Saturday, and their frequent phone conversations skirted around the issues most important to both of them. His life seemed empty without seeing her, but what could he say that wouldn't hurt her more than he already had?

* * *

When he got to the church, he was surprised to see Betty Jo's car in the parking lot. She never worked on Saturday, not even as a volunteer. It was her cleaning and shopping day, and she always kept to her schedule.

He found her in the office, busy talking on the phone.

"Oh, Reverend Mac," she said, breaking off her call. "I left my list here, so I thought I might as well do my phoning here."

"That's fine," he said, assuming her calls were personal.

"It's church business, really," she explained. "I'm calling people to remind them about 'Haircuts for Hunger.'"

As much as he'd thought about Jenny all week, he'd forgotten her project to raise money and collect canned goods for flood victims. The beauty shop would be open all afternoon. Anyone who wanted a haircut could donate as little as a can of peas or as much cash as they felt moved to contribute.

He ran his hand through his hair, surprised at how shaggy it was. He'd intended to get to the barbershop all week, but he never seemed to have the time.

"Jenny and Charlene and that new girl—I forget her name—are all volunteering their time," Betty Jo said enthusiastically. "I'm going to drive my neighbor there. She's eighty-eight and doesn't get out much, so it will be a real treat for her. She really can't afford the price of a haircut, but I'm sure she'll be able to contribute a can of food."

"That's nice," Mac said, hardly hearing what his secretary said.

He couldn't help remembering the haircut Jenny had given him when he first came to town. Even then he'd felt there was something special about her.

He sighed and went into his office, explaining to Betty Jo that he wanted to go over his sermon for tomorrow. He laid it in front of him on the desk, but he couldn't seem to focus on the words. He felt like a man who'd left something undone.

Jenny couldn't have been more eager for "Haircuts for Hunger." She didn't kid herself. It would be hard work. She'd been exhausted after giving so many free cuts in Dillard, and it had taken a couple of days for her arm and shoulder to get back to normal. Still, she hoped people would line up around the block. She wanted to donate a ton of food to people who desperately needed it, but she also wanted to be too busy to think about Mac.

She hadn't seen him that week, but in a way that was good. She'd been terribly busy, but she didn't want him to know what she was doing until she was sure of success.

She loved him more than she could express, but she also valued the way he'd made her reexamine her life. Whatever happened between them when he heard her news, she was going to do something to change things and go forward.

"You have to get in touch with your own feelings before you can begin to heal," Sandy had told her after a support group session.

Jenny hadn't paid much attention when she'd said it, but now she was beginning to understand what it meant. She hadn't wanted to fall in love with Mac. He complicated her life as well as his own. She'd needed him to be stronger than she was and not let love take hold between them. Now it was too late for that.

The shop wasn't busy that morning, just a couple of

perms and some color retouches. Jenny took that as a good sign. Regular customers were waiting to come that afternoon, hopefully bringing friends and relatives with them. She badly wanted her food-raising project to be a big success, not for her sake but because the need was so great.

Charlene put two clothes baskets by the checkout counter, and Nadine made a sign and decorated a box with a slot in the top for cash donations. Their excitement was contagious, and Jenny pushed thoughts of Mac out of her mind to get ready for the big afternoon.

"Wow!" Nadine silently mouthed when people started streaming into the store, filling the baskets with food before the haircuts even started.

Instead of the can or two Jenny had expected, people came with bags of groceries, fresh produce, paper products and staples. Many added a cash donation to their food donation. All the seats in the waiting area were filled and women were milling around waiting for their haircuts. Charlene had to use a sign-up sheet to tell whose turn it was.

With so many people waiting, Jenny felt rushed but gratified. She made an extra effort to do her very best with each cut.

Mac came late and was the last person in the line for haircuts. He sat down in her chair before she could call his name.

"You don't mind, do you?" he asked in a quiet voice.

"I'm here for anyone who contributes to the food drive," she said, trying to pretend that he was just another customer.

"Afraid I didn't get to the supermarket, but I put my check in the box."

She wrapped a paper strip around his neck and tied a cape

around him, gestures that seemed intimate with him even though she did the same thing dozens of times every week.

"I'll be back in a minute," she said, hurrying to the back and drinking from a bottle of water she'd left there.

Breathing deeply several times and forcing herself to calm down, she was still dismayed by the tremors in her hands. She tried to blame her shakiness on the afternoon's hectic pace, but she knew it was a reaction to Mac. She'd wanted desperately to see him, but not here, not as a customer.

Slowly she returned to her station. He was waiting patiently, his eyes focused on something far away.

"Now, how would you like it?" she asked, fiddling with her scissors to cover her nervousness.

"You did a great job the last time you cut it," he said. "I'll leave it up to you."

She was going to botch it. She couldn't treat him as just another client, but what choice did she have? She combed through his dark brown hair, surprised by how silky it seemed when her fingers brushed against it.

"Well, here goes," she said more to herself than him.

His eyes followed her movements in the mirror, but she tried not to notice. She'd given a thousand haircuts, but this one was different. This was the man she loved.

Nadine went by her station and said goodbye for the day, congratulating her on how much food they'd accumulated.

"Thanks for all your help," Jenny said, wishing she would stay until Mac left.

She wanted to be alone with him, but not in the shop, not now when she still didn't know whether her plan would be successful.

Charlene came out before Jenny finished Mac's haircut.

"It was a wonderful turnout," she enthused. "Would

you mind locking up when you're done? I have to admit I'm exhausted."

"I'll see to it," Jenny said. "Thanks so much for donating the shop and all your time."

"The food can stay here until Monday, but maybe you'd better take the cash box with you," the proprietor said. "I never like to leave a lot of money lying around, especially when it isn't mine."

"I'll take care of it," Jenny promised.

She finished Mac's haircut in silence, tortured by his nearness and all the unsaid things between them. His eyes followed her, but he didn't say anything until she asked whether his hair looked okay.

"It doesn't matter," he admitted. "I only came to see you."

"There are easier ways to do that."

"I suppose."

"I have to clean up. Mom will have dinner waiting," she said.

"I'll help."

"You really don't need to."

"At least let me stay until you lock up. The cash in that box could be pretty tempting," he argued.

"This is Pleasantville," she said more sharply than she'd intended.

"Yes. It was only an excuse to wait here with you."

"If you like, you can take the whole box with you until I have time to count it."

"I'll put it in the church safe if you want me to. That was a wonderful thing you did today, Jenny. You gave a lot of people an opportunity to feel good about themselves, and the donations will mean a lot."

She didn't want to be thanked, especially not by Mac.

Everything he said reminded her of the obstacles between them. She could hardly endure being with him but not *with him*.

"You've worked so hard. Can I take you to dinner?" he asked.

"Thanks, but I'm beat. I think I'll just go home and collapse."

"I'll leave then," he said in a neutral tone. "Thank you for all you've done, Jenny."

She thrust the donation box at him but didn't follow him to the door as he left. She wasn't ready to tell him what she was trying to do, but she wasn't good at keeping secrets. Above all, she didn't want him to think she was trying to entrap him.

Mac knew he'd blown it, but he didn't know what he'd expected to accomplish. Getting Jenny to cut his hair had been a bad idea. Asking her out for dinner at such short notice after a hard day was probably a worse move. How did she feel about him now? Was she angry? Hurt? Disappointed in him? Probably all that and more.

He tossed the box on the passenger seat of the car and looked up at the sky. It had grown darker since he went into the shop, and he prayed that the rain wouldn't cause more flooding. The state had more than it could handle cleaning up from the other summer storms.

The first raindrops spattered on his dusty car in a polka-dot pattern, and he barely had time to get behind the wheel before the sky let loose. He wasn't a man prone to glum moods, but his spirits had never been lower.

"Jenny, Jenny, Jenny," he whispered to himself.

The clouds hanging over the two of them were darker and denser than the storm clouds threatening Pleasantville.

What could a man do when love clouded everything else in his life?

In a moment of life-changing clarity, he knew what he had to do.

Chapter Nineteen

Jenny was beginning to understand what the dog days of summer were. The weather was hot and humid, and no one was moving more than they had to. Charlene decided to close the shop for a week after their successful "Haircuts for Hunger," giving both of her employees a week of paid vacation. Jenny appreciated her boss's generosity. She had places to go and things to do.

Something was up in the Kincaid house. There was an air of excitement when her mother and sister got home from work Thursday evening. Sandy fed Toby while Gloria called for a pizza delivery, not something they usually did on a weeknight.

"Luke is coming for dinner," her sister said. "We have something to tell you."

It was becoming commonplace for Luke to spend time with Sandy, and Jenny found herself liking him quite a bit. Besides being nice to her sister, he was patient and kind with Toby. He often included him in restaurant meals, although the little guy could be a pip in public situations.

Jenny believed Luke would do well teaching and

coaching the high school football team. He was soft-spoken and a good listener, and he had a gift for getting along with people. Most importantly, he doted on Sandy and treated her with respect.

Luke and the pizza arrived at the same time and they settled down at the kitchen table while Toby hammered on the high chair tray with a plastic spoon.

Jenny and her mother started eating, but Sandy and Luke just looked at each other. Something was on their minds, and it must have been important because neither of them paid any attention to the pizza.

"We have something to tell you," Sandy began.

"I'd like the honor of marrying your daughter, Mrs. Kincaid," Luke said formally. "I know we haven't known each other very long, but we both feel that this is right for us."

"We're going to wait until Christmas," Sandy said.

Gloria seemed speechless, although Jenny didn't think she could possibly be as surprised as she acted. She got up and hugged her sister, then congratulated Luke with a sisterly hug.

"I'm so happy for both of you," Jenny said as her mother wiped tears from her eyes.

Although she'd never consciously thought of her family as a burden, a great weight seemed to fall from her shoulders. Sandy would have someone to share her life with, and Toby would have a daddy to help care for him. Her mother was spending more time with George than with her daughters, so Jenny felt freer than she ever would have imagined.

She wasn't quite ready to tell them her news, but when she was, it wouldn't greatly affect their lives. That was good.

Toby shrieked with pleasure as he sent his spoon

soaring over the table. Dinnertime was over for him. Luke got up to wash his face and free him from the high chair while Sandy beamed at both of them. They seemed like a family already, and it was time for Jenny to get on with her life.

Mac was restless. He'd made his sermon notes, torn them up and rewritten them. The pile of books on his desk didn't have any answers to his dilemma, and for once in his life Mac couldn't focus on the printed word.

He'd prayed so much lately that he wryly thought the Lord must be tired of hearing from him. Now he was certain he had to make his own decision.

He wanted to see Jenny.

He desperately, fervently wanted to see Jenny.

But before he could call her, he had to put his house in order. He had to cement his decision about his future.

He stared at the phone for a long time, wondering how to put his feelings into words. He would never reject the Lord, but he knew now what his true calling was. He punched in a number and worked his way through the recorded messages that made phoning an obstacle course.

At last he took a deep breath and began the conversation that would change his life.

Jenny didn't have to go to the shop during her week off, but she had promised to keep an eye on it while Charlene visited her sister in Kentucky. She was too restless to settle down after Sandy's announcement, and Mac was at the hospital with an elderly member of the congregation who'd just undergone heart surgery. In fact, everyone she knew seemed to be busy this evening.

She opened the front door of the shop and immediately

thought of a few jobs that could be done. All the mirrors could use a good polishing, and a new set of posters showing hairstyles had arrived last week. This was a good time to switch them with the old ones displayed in frames on the wall of the waiting area.

Locking the door behind her, she started to work, at the same time going over all the plans she'd set in motion so far that week. She'd gathered references, filled in a multitude of forms and visited the school. She was assured of financial aid in the form of a loan, but her own savings would get her off to a good start. Now all she had to do was wait for an acceptance letter, which the admissions counselor said might not come for a couple of months, depending on how many applications they had to process for the next term.

She was going to train to be an LPN, a licensed practical nurse. The fifty-mile commute every day would be tedious, but her excitement more than overcame any obstacles. Maybe someday she could go on to become a registered nurse, but for now she felt that she'd made a giant step forward.

A tiny voice in the back of her head told her that she could be a worthy helpmate, no matter where Mac was called to go.

She was startled by a knock on the door and cautious about unlocking it until she saw Mac standing outside.

"I didn't mean to scare you," he said as he came in.

"That's okay. I just wasn't expecting anyone."

"Your mother told me you were here."

"Mac, I have to tell you—"

"Jenny, I have to tell you—"

They spoke almost in unison, then laughed nervously.

"You first," Mac said, reaching out and taking her hand.

"No, my news will keep. What do you want to tell me?"

"I called the head of the mission board today."

Her heart sank, and she prepared herself for bad news. Mac would be leaving before she was ready to go with him.

"I told him to take my name off their list. I've found my calling here in West Virginia."

"You're going to stay in Pleasantville?"

"I don't know about that. I may not be asked to stay on here, but there are other churches with needs as great or greater. Now what's your news?"

A current ran between their clasped hands, and she found the courage to tell him what she'd done—and why.

"I've applied to become a nurse. I wanted to be worthy of going with you if you were called to a foreign mission."

He looked so stunned that she was afraid she'd assumed too much. Maybe he wouldn't want to take her with him—but that didn't matter now because he wasn't going.

"You did that to be with me?" he asked as though he couldn't quite believe it.

"You decided to stay here to be with me?" She was trembling with happiness, not sure this was really happening.

"I love you, Jenny. I want you to be with me forever."

"I love you too with all my heart."

He took her in his arms and bent his head for a long, sweet kiss.

"Well, here we are again," he said in a soft, teasing voice. "I can't say I fell in love with you in this beauty parlor, but I'd never seen anyone as sweet and beautiful as you are. Here." He led her to the chair where she'd first cut his hair and asked her to sit.

To her immense surprise and pleasure, he got down on his knees in front of her.

"Jenny, will you marry me?"

"Nothing could make me happier."

Her heart pounded with joy as he stood and took her in his arms.

Together they stood and looked into each other's eyes.

"Do you really want to be a nurse?" he asked.

"Yes, I'm ready for a change in my life."

"I'm so proud of you. I'll do anything I can to help you achieve that. Now that I think of it, you may need a career to support both of us. My future is none too certain."

"I can't imagine any congregation not wanting you as their minister."

"You may be slightly biased," he said, sounding happier than she'd ever heard him.

"I'm hugely biased. I think you're the most wonderful man in the world, Reverend Arnett."

"Mac to you, my darling."

Her eyes were moist, tears of sheer joy clouding her vision.

"I think we have people to tell," he said. "My parents will think they've gone to Heaven when they hear their errant son is finally getting married."

"You're not so old!"

"No, but my mother has been thinking orange blossoms and wedding cake since I had my first date in high school."

"Oh, that reminds me. Sandy and Luke are engaged. My mother will be overwhelmed by so much good news in one day."

"I think she'll handle it just fine," he said. "Shall we lock up here and go find out?"

They left, walking with their arms around each other, so lost in the happiness of the moment that they couldn't say "I love you" often enough.

Several weeks later Mac was working at his desk when he looked up and was surprised to see George Darlington standing in the open doorway to his office. Betty Jo had taken the day off, and Mac hadn't expected to see anyone today.

"I don't want to disturb you if you're working," George said.

"You're welcome any time," Mac said, altogether pleased with the good working relationship they had.

"I want you to know that the church council made a decision about your tenure before you and Jenny announced you were getting married."

"Oh?"

"We didn't think there was any hurry in telling you, but a man planning to get married needs to know he has a job."

Mac waited, surprised by how much he wanted to stay with his congregation in Pleasantville. They'd welcomed him as one of them and willingly helped with everyday concerns and volunteering to help with the flood disaster. He already felt that he was part of a church family. The president of the congregation didn't sound like a man about to fire him, but Mac wouldn't breathe easily until he heard his news.

"We want to offer you a permanent position," George said beaming. "You've given the church a new direction, and we really appreciate your leadership and dedication. It's probably the first time the church council had agreed on something one hundred percent."

Mac thought of all the needs within the congregation

and the poverty of surrounding communities. The Lord had given him a mission and it was all around him. He didn't hesitate to accept George's offer.

Epilogue

Jenny felt oddly calm, but her sister was a whirlwind of activity, putting the finishing touches on Jenny's wedding dress and fussing with her bouquet. Mac's father was officiating, and afterward the reception would be in the church community room. They'd wanted to keep it as simple as possible, but things had a way of spiraling out of control. Mac had invited the entire congregation, and the women of the church had come forward to supply food and help.

"How can you be so calm?" Sandy asked, checking her maid-of-honor dress in the mirror of the church room designated as a dressing room for the wedding party.

"What should I be doing?"

"Well—something."

They both broke down in laughter.

"You're the calmest bride I've ever seen," Sandy said.

"Inside I'm a churning mass of nerves," Jenny said.

"Oh, I almost forgot. The mail came before Luke drove

me here. I thought you might want to see this even though it is your wedding day."

"It's from the school," she said, staring at the return address.

"Well, open it," Sandy urged.

"What if they've turned me down?"

"Then you'll try some other school."

"There aren't any others, not close enough to drive to every day. Maybe I shouldn't have applied."

"Of course, you should have. And you know what, someday I'll get my teaching certificate. Luke says being able to take courses on the Internet will help a lot. He totally supports me. So open it."

Jenny slid her finger under the flap to open it and pulled out a sheath of papers topped by a letter. After reading for a moment, she smiled broadly.

"I'm in!"

"Wonderful!" Sandy hugged her and snatched the letter to read it herself.

"You have a good chance of getting a scholarship too. Look, they've sent you about a hundred papers to fill out," her sister said.

Jenny's heart was singing. How could one day contain so much happiness?

Through a window, Jenny could see a brisk wind whipping fallen leaves across the parking lot, but the weather was mild for late October. Guests were arriving in groups and clusters, but Jenny didn't feel any of the nervousness she'd seen in other brides. Kayla and Kate, her other two attendants, had already left to await their walk down the aisle, and Sandy gave her a final careful hug.

If the wedding had grown larger than originally planned, it was because they couldn't bear to leave out close friends. Mac had called on attendants from out of town, but Luke, as a future brother-in-law, was one of the ushers. Her mother's boyfriend, George, had proudly agreed to escort the bride down the aisle.

Jenny loved Mac so much that she could hardly believe they would be united for life.

Once the ceremony began, she and Mac stood in front of his silver-haired father. Mac took her hand as they exchanged their vows in clear, steady voices.

She was floating on a cloud of happiness, unable to take her eyes from the handsome man beside her. He was wearing a dark suit and a gleaming white shirt with a dark burgundy bow tie, a touch she found endearing. Was this really happening to her?

"I now pronounce you man and wife," his father's voice rang forth.

Mac took her in his arms and lightly brushed her lips, then deepened their kiss until organ music parted them for the rush down the aisle.

Well-wishers slowly paraded by the reception line, and Toby proved to be a natural at greeting people as he let his little hand be grasped again and again from the security of his mother's arms. Gloria was on her third hanky, still dabbing at her eyes from time to time as she was overwhelmed by happiness.

She and Mac didn't have words for each other until the last guest paraded by and went to the room where the wedding feast would soon be served.

"Mrs. Arnett, how can I tell you how much I love you?" Mac asked, bending close to her ear and touching a strand of honey-blond hair.

"You're welcome to try as much as you like," she said.

She moved into his arms and knew that home would always be where Mac was.

* * * * *

Dear Reader,

The people and places of West Virginia are near and dear to me, after having spent many years in that fine state. Thank you for sharing in Mac and Jenny's story. Theirs is a love that just needed time to blossom like the dogwood that flowers during an Appalachian spring.

Love takes time, and with the Lord's help all things are possible. Both Mac and Jenny learned this lesson. I hope you have your faith, family and friends to guide you on a similar path.

I love to hear from readers. Please e-mail me at: psharc@gmail.com.

Best,

Pam Andrews

QUESTIONS FOR DISCUSSION

1. What characteristics make Mac a good minister?

2. How has your faith helped you through a time of loss?

3. How did Jenny use her God-given talents to help others? How are you able to help others?

4. How is your community weathering tough economic times?

5. Have you and a loved one ever faced an uncertain future together just as Jenny and Mac do? How did you resolve your situation?

6. Jenny and Mac come from very different but supportive families. Another family is your church family. What kind of comfort have you received from your church family in a time of need?

7. Have you lived in one place your whole life? Would you be willing to move for love? Why or why not?

8. Have you ever had a time when your belief in the Lord helped you discover your talents?

9. How did Jenny feel about working in the flood-stricken town? Have you ever been in a similar situation to help others?

10. In your own life, have you been able to let go of past hurts and move on? Why or why not?

11. How do you feel the Bible verse relates to what happens in this story?

12. On a lighter note, have you ever gotten a bad haircut? Was it a problem of how you communicated with the hairdresser?

Here's a sneak preview of
THE RANCHER'S PROMISE
by Jillian Hart
Available in June 2010
from Love Inspired

"So, are you back to stay?" Justin's deep voice hid any shades of emotion. Was he fishing for information or was he finally about to say "I told you so"?

"I'll probably go back to teaching in Dallas, but things could change. I'll just have to wait and see." The things in life she used to think were so important no longer mattered. Standing on her own two feet, building a life for herself, healing her wounds—that did.

"And this man you married?" he asked. "Did he leave you or did you leave him?"

"He threw me out." She waited for Justin's reaction. Surely a man with that severe a frown on his face was about to take delight in the irony. She'd turned down Justin's love, and her husband of five years had thrown away hers. If she were Justin, she would want her off his land.

"You were nothing but honest with me back then." He leaned against the railing, the wind raking his dark hair, and a different emotion passed across his hard countenance. "I was the one who never listened. I loved you so much, I don't think I could hear anything but what I wanted."

"I loved you, too. I wish I could have been different for you." Helpless, she took another step toward the driveway. She didn't know how to thank him. He could be treating her a lot worse right now, and she would deserve it. "Goodbye, Justin."

"I suppose you need a job?"

"I'll figure out something." Need a job? No, she was frantic for one. How did she tell him the truth?

Find out in THE RANCHER'S PROMISE
Available June 2010 from Love Inspired

Love Inspired

Bestselling author

JILLIAN HART

brings you another heartwarming story
from

the

GRANGER
FAMILY
RANCH

Rancher Justin Granger hasn't seen his high school sweetheart
since she rode out of town with his heart. Now she's back, with
sadness in her eyes, seeking a job as his cook and housekeeper.
He agrees but is determined to avoid her...until he discovers
that her big dream has always been him!

The Rancher's Promise

*Available June
wherever books are sold.*

Steeple
Hill®

www.SteepleHill.com

LI87601

LARGER-PRINT BOOKS!

GET 2 FREE
LARGER-PRINT NOVELS
PLUS 2 FREE
MYSTERY GIFTS

Larger-print novels are now available...

YES! Please send me 2 FREE LARGER-PRINT Love Inspired® novels and my 2 FREE mystery gifts (gifts are worth about $10). After receiving them, if I don't wish to receive any more books, I can return the shipping statement marked "cancel". If I don't cancel, I will receive 6 brand-new novels every month and be billed just $4.74 per book in the U.S. or $5.24 per book in Canada. That's a saving of over 20% off the cover price. It's quite a bargain! Shipping and handling is just 50¢ per book in the U.S. and 75¢ per book in Canada.* I understand that accepting the 2 free books and gifts places me under no obligation to buy anything. I can always return a shipment and cancel at any time. Even if I never buy another book, the two free books and gifts are mine to keep forever.

122 IDN E4KN   322 IDN E4KY

Name	(PLEASE PRINT)	
Address		Apt. #
City	State/Prov.	Zip/Postal Code

Signature (if under 18, a parent or guardian must sign)

Mail to **Steeple Hill Reader Service:**
IN U.S.A.: P.O. Box 1867, Buffalo, NY 14240-1867
IN CANADA: P.O. Box 609, Fort Erie, Ontario L2A 5X3

**Are you a current subscriber to Love Inspired books
and want to receive the larger-print edition?
Call 1-800-873-8635 or visit www.morefreebooks.com.**

* Terms and prices subject to change without notice. Prices do not include applicable taxes. Sales tax applicable in N.Y. Canadian residents will be charged applicable provincial taxes and GST. Offer not valid in Quebec. This offer is limited to one order per household. All orders subject to approval. Credit or debit balances in a customer's account(s) may be offset by any other outstanding balance owed by or to the customer. Please allow 4 to 6 weeks for delivery. Offer available while quantities last.

Your Privacy: Steeple Hill Books is committed to protecting your privacy. Our Privacy Policy is available online at www.SteepleHill.com or upon request from the Reader Service. From time to time we make our lists of customers available to reputable third parties who may have a product or service of interest to you. If you would prefer we not share your name and address, please check here. ☐

Help us get it right—We strive for accurate, respectful and relevant communications. To clarify or modify your communication preferences, visit us at www.ReaderService.com/consumerschoice.

LILP10

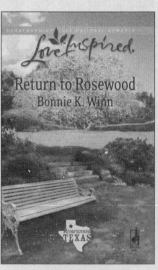

TITLES AVAILABLE NEXT MONTH

Available May 25, 2010

THE RANCHER'S PROMISE
The Granger Family Ranch
Jillian Hart

RETURN TO ROSEWOOD
Rosewood, Texas
Bonnie K. Winn

COWBOY FOR KEEPS
Men of Mule Hollow
Debra Clopton

THE PASTOR TAKES A WIFE
Anna Schmidt

STEADFAST SOLDIER
Wings of Refuge
Cheryl Wyatt

THE HEART'S SONG
Winnie Griggs